"I'm sorry it's been so long, Georgie, I really am," he said.

She attempted to tease, but her words fell flat. "You know whose fault that is."

"Mine. I know. And I regret it." He paused.

"Yet you're here now." She made no move toward him. No kiss on the cheek or hug in welcome—not that their friendship had ever been the kind that involved physical contact beyond the socially polite. There had always been an unspoken "no touching" barrier between them.

Back in the day, when Wil had smiled, there had been a hint of a dimple in his left cheek that, in spite of herself, she'd always found appealing. He wasn't smiling now. Georgia didn't smile, either. Once, they'd been such close friends they'd joked they could read each other's minds. Now she could see in his eyes that he knew he'd hurt her by the way he'd dumped her. She wasn't inclined to be forgiving. But this was Wil and he had sought her out. She had to give him a hearing.

"I need your help," he said, his voice gruff.

Dear Reader,

When people celebrate their wedding anniversaries on social media, I'm surprised at how many longtime couples say, "I married my best friend."

In both my own life and in my books, I've been a fan of the quick flare of flames rather than the slow burn. I've championed love at first sight (my husband and I decided to spend our lives together after three days) rather than friendship evolving into love. But what about all those happy marriages between best friends?

I realized "friends to lovers" was the way to go in *Second Chance with the Single Dad*. Girl-next-door schoolteacher Georgia Lang and handsome self-made millionaire Wil Hudson go way back as "just friends." They know each other so well they claim to read each other's thoughts. But not everyone wishes the platonic friends well and the friendship ends abruptly and painfully. What happens when Wil becomes a single dad to adorable baby Nina and asks Georgia for help? Can they salvage the friendship—and perhaps acknowledge the tiny flickering flames that just might have been there all along?

I loved bringing these two together so they could find the true love that had been waiting there for them to discover. I hope you enjoy their story!

Warm regards,

Kandy

Second Chance with the Single Dad

Kandy Shepherd

HARLEQUIN® ROMANCE

Recycling programs
for this product may
not exist in your area.

ISBN-13: 978-1-335-49924-0

Second Chance with the Single Dad

First North American publication 2019

Copyright © 2019 by Kandy Shepherd

 HARLEQUIN®

™ www.Harlequin.com

Printed in U.S.A.

Kandy Shepherd swapped a career as a magazine editor for a life writing romance. She lives on a small farm in the Blue Mountains near Sydney, Australia, with her husband, daughter and lots of pets. She believes in love at first sight and real-life romance—they worked for her! Kandy loves to hear from her readers. Visit her at kandyshepherd.com.

Books by Kandy Shepherd

Harlequin Romance

Sydney Brides

Gift-Wrapped in Her Wedding Dress
Crown Prince's Chosen Bride
The Bridesmaid's Baby Bump

A Diamond in Her Stocking
From Paradise...to Pregnant!
Hired by the Brooding Billionaire
Greek Tycoon's Mistletoe Proposal
Conveniently Wed to the Greek
Stranded with Her Greek Tycoon
Best Man and the Runaway Bride

Visit the Author Profile page
at Harlequin.com for more titles.

To my precious daughter, Lucy. You're grown up now, but your adorable baby self was the inspiration for every baby I've ever written, including the enchanting little girl in this story. And of course you're my go-to for all matters equine!

Praise for
Kandy Shepherd

"I was drawn into this fast-paced story by engaging dialogue, lively banter, and the drama.... Passionate, touching and immensely satisfying and I definitely would recommend it to romance lovers!"

—*Goodreads* on *Conveniently Wed to the Greek*

CHAPTER ONE

W<small>IL</small> H<small>UDSON</small> <small>WAS</small> a handsome, handsome man. Georgia Lang had recognised his exceptional good looks from day one of their friendship. What red-blooded female wouldn't? But she had never allowed herself to acknowledge even a flutter of attraction to him.

It was way safer to be 'just friends' with a man who attracted women as effortlessly as gorgeous Wil did—and discarded them as readily. Especially when she was just an ordinary girl, attractive enough, but hardly a winner in the head-turning stakes. Nothing like the women Wil dated. *Girl next door* was the way people described her. On self-doubting days, she wondered if that was shorthand for distinctly unexciting. Most of the time she embraced the label as a good fit.

As Wil's *girl next door* pal, his buddy, his good mate from university days, she'd watched as his glamorous girlfriends came and went while their friendship endured. To be sure, it had ebbed and flowed. They'd always seen more of each other when they'd been between relationships; there had been moments when she'd wondered if they could be more than friends. But, fearing rejection, she hadn't dared suggest it; he hadn't either, and they'd each dived back into the dating pool.

But all that had been before Wil's whirlwind marriage. After he'd wed, none of their group of friends had seen much of him. They'd seen him even less after his wife had left him. Georgia hadn't seen him at all. He'd ghosted her—just stopped all contact without explanation. Not a call, not a text, not even a 'like' on social media. She'd seen him interviewed on television, he'd become a reluctant go-to spokesperson for the young generation of millionaires. But he might as well have been a ghost for all the personal contact she'd had with him.

Now, just days into the new year, he stood at the doorstep of the North Sydney apartment she shared with two other schoolteachers. She was so taken aback to find him there she had to clutch at the door frame for support. *Wil.* Her heart started a furious beating. *How she'd missed him.*

Incredulous delight flooded through her at

seeing the friend she'd painfully accepted was no longer part of her life. She started to blurt out her pleasure at his unexpected appearance, wish him the happiest of new years. To tell him she was moving house and he was just in time to help her lift some heavy boxes of books and she'd reward him with the cookies she knew were his favourite. But she held herself back. This Wil wasn't her best friend. She hadn't deserved how he'd treated her. This Wil seemed like a stranger.

If it had been any other guy she might have shrieked about what a wreck she looked, in shorts and a past-its-use-by-date vest top, no make-up, hair rioting every which way from the January summer humidity. But she'd never worried about her appearance with Wil; she doubted he'd ever noticed what she'd worn.

But she'd always noticed him. The impact of his good looks hit her afresh—tall, broad-shouldered, in dark jeans and a white T-shirt that showcased his athletic physique. For a long moment she stared at him as he met her gaze through narrowed eyes. What was he doing here? Why now?

'Georgie,' he said slowly, his voice as deep and resonant as it had always been. His eyes searched her face, acknowledging that it had been a long time between meetings, waiting for her reaction. She met his gaze unflinchingly, drinking in the sight of him.

He was the same, but not quite the same. Wil had always been well groomed in a clean-shaven, country-boy kind of way. Now he was a few days away from a shave and stubble shadowed his jaw. His dark hair, longer than he used to wear it, fell unkempt over his forehead. Fine lines scored the corners of his eyes, the colour of bittersweet chocolate. At twenty-eight, a year older than her, he seemed somehow…weary. Perhaps making so much money so quickly did that for you, she thought cynically. Maybe it had also made him think he'd outgrown his old friends.

'It's been two years,' she said at last, determined not to let a note of accusation edge her voice but failing dismally. Laughter and good-humoured teasing had been the keynotes of their friendship but she couldn't find it in herself to summon them up. It had hurt, the way he had so abruptly discarded their friendship of six years' duration.

Friendship not just diminished—as did happen when friends met 'The One'—but extinguished. As if those years had meant nothing when he had finally fallen in love. As if she had just been a convenient prop, of no further use in his new life. *Good old Georgia—no longer required.* She couldn't hide that hurt. Couldn't pretend it didn't matter.

And Wil wasn't fooled for a moment. 'I'm sorry it's been so long, Georgie, I really am,' he said.

She attempted to tease but her words fell flat. 'You know whose fault that is.'

'Mine. I know. And I regret it.' He paused.

'Yet you're here now.' She made no move towards him. No kiss on the cheek or hug in welcome—not that their friendship had ever been the kind that involved physical contact beyond the socially polite. There had always been an unspoken 'no touching' barrier between them.

Back in the day, when Wil had smiled there had been a hint of a dimple in his left cheek that, in spite of herself, she'd always found appealing. He wasn't smiling now. Georgia didn't smile either. Once they'd been such close friends they'd joked they could read each other's minds. Now she could see in his eyes that he knew he'd hurt her by the way he'd dumped her. She wasn't inclined to be forgiving. But this was Wil and he had sought her out. She had to give him a hearing.

'I need your help,' he said, his voice gruff.

Georgia could tell the effort it took for him to force out those words. Once she would have immediately jumped in to ask what she could do for him. Good old Georgia would have cancelled prior engagements. Rearranged schedules. Bent over backwards to accommodate him—far more, she realised, than he had ever done for her as his good friend. Now she remained with her feet planted firmly at the threshold. 'I heard you and your wife had divorced.'

Angie, tiny, blonde, with a waif-like air that hadn't hidden her calculating eyes. None of the girls in their friendship group had been taken in by her. Not so the guys. But none had been so smitten as Wil.

'Yes,' he said shortly.

Georgia crossed her arms across her chest. 'I'm no longer available as number one shoulder to cry on when you break up with a woman.' *Not one word from him in two years.* 'I'm afraid my give-a-damn quota has expired,' she said.

Only a tightening of his lips let her know that her words had met their target. He cleared his throat once, then again. 'Angie…she… Angie's dead,' he said.

Georgia clutched a hand to her heart. 'What?' She expelled just the one word, tinged with disbelief. But Wil's bleak expression told her to believe him. 'When? How?'

'Car accident in the Blue Mountains. New Year's Eve. She…she died the next day in hospital. Three days ago.'

'Oh, Wil, that's dreadful. I'm so sorry.' She remembered all the bitchy thoughts she'd had about Wil's fluffy little wife. Regretted every one of them. Also regretted the just-spoken 'not giving a damn' remark. Angie was—had been—twenty-seven, the same age as her. Frighteningly young to die. 'I'm sorry,' she said again, not certain what else she could say. 'Come in. Please. How can I help?'

She stepped aside to let him through the door. Apologised for the half-packed boxes around the place. Led him through to the living room, glad neither of her flatmates was home. Opened her mouth to offer him coffee. Maybe something stronger, even though it was only mid-morning. But Wil spoke first.

'I have a baby. A little girl called Nina.'

'Oh.' Another stab of hurt shafted through her, that he hadn't cared to tell her something so momentous. 'I didn't know you were a father.'

'Neither did I,' he said.

Georgia was too shell-shocked to find an immediate reply. 'What do you mean?' she eventually choked out. 'How could you not know?'

'Angie didn't tell me. I wasn't aware she was pregnant, let alone that she'd had a baby. We weren't in contact after our short marriage ended. Only through divorce lawyers.'

Yet she was pregnant? Break-up sex perhaps. Georgia couldn't ask. She'd heard the marriage had lasted less than six months. 'Why didn't she tell you?'

Wil swore under his breath. 'I don't know. To punish me. To… Hell. I don't know why. Or if she ever intended to tell me. But she put my name on the birth certificate.'

The Angie that Georgia remembered would have milked a guy for all he had in child support. She'd had dollar signs flashing in her eyes when she'd met successful, wealthy Wil. He'd been an amateur inventor who had made a lot of money through patents after he'd appeared on a television show. 'Then how—?'

'A social worker from Katoomba Hospital in the Blue Mountains contacted me on New Year's Day. Told me my ex-wife had died. After the accident, she regained consciousness briefly and told the social worker she wanted me to take custody of the baby. It…it came from out of the blue.'

Wil a father. Now Georgia realised her old friend didn't just look weary. He looked dazed, as if his world had turned upside down, as if he wasn't sure where to place his feet so he wouldn't topple over. And he had reached out to *her*.

Wil had missed Georgia's friendship. He hadn't realised quite how much until just now when she'd opened the door to him, not with her customary wide, open smile but tight-lipped and guarded. The full impact of how he had hurt her had hit him like a blow to the gut.

But two years ago, his first loyalty had been to Angie. She had been pretty, sexy and fun—in the beginning. There'd been a vulnerability to her too that had drawn him to her. But she'd got very demanding very quickly. When Angie had begged him not to see his close female friend—not even to say goodbye—he'd had to go along with it. That was what a guy did for his woman. Besides, he'd learned very early that to disagree with Angie wasn't worth it. No matter how large a gap Georgia had left in his life.

When the blinkers had come off, when he'd realised that Angie was too damaged for a normal relationship, he'd cut his losses and ended it very quickly. His gentlemanly instinct had been to let Angie tell people she'd been the one to leave. It had probably been doomed from the start—two people with troubled pasts drawn to each other, he wanting to rescue her, she deciding to blame him for all that was wrong with her life.

But that was in the past. Angie was tragically gone. And he'd found he was a father.

Now his lovely friend of such long standing stood near to him, cheeks flushed, her chestnut hair a riot of waves around her face, her blue eyes warm with both sympathy and a shocked surprise.

'Was the baby injured in the accident?' she asked.

'Thankfully not. Angie's sister was babysitting that night.'

'Thank heaven.' Georgia shook her head as if to clear her thoughts. 'I'm having trouble taking this in. I can't imagine how you must have felt at such news.'

Wil briefly closed his eyes at the intensity of his relief that she hadn't turned him away. Breathed in his friend's sweet scent, immediately familiar, immediately comforting. *Georgia*.

'Nothing could have prepared me for it,' he said.

He still couldn't articulate his shock and disbelief at the call from the hospital. Angie's tragic death had been enough to cope with, without the news of his unexpected paternity.

Then he'd had to deal with the anger he'd felt towards his ex for keeping him out of the loop. The doubt that the child was his.

'What did you do?'

'Drove straight to Katoomba. Met with the social worker. Met…met my daughter.'

My daughter. Emotion swamped him as he remembered seeing the impossibly little girl in the social worker's arms. How she had looked up at him with dark solemn eyes—his eyes— then reached over one tiny starfish hand to grip his finger strong and hard. He struggled not to let that emotion show on his face. Not to Georgia. Sensible, steady Georgia to whom he had been so careful never to reveal who he was, what he was, for fear she would turn away from him.

'How…how old is she?' He could see Georgia was struggling with the fact he had a child. He'd only had a few days to get used to the idea himself. But already he thought of himself as a father, determined to give that tiny scrap of humanity everything in life that had been denied him.

'Seven months.'

'That's very young. What are you going to do?'

'Go get her today,' he said without hesitation.

'What do you mean?'

'Angie's sister in Katoomba is kicking up a fuss. Seems to think she has a claim on Nina. She doesn't, of course. Legally she hasn't got a leg to stand on. But the sooner I have Nina with me, the better.'

Georgia's blue eyes widened. 'You mean you intend to bring Nina up by yourself?'

'She's my responsibility. I'm heading up to the Blue Mountains to pick her up and take her home.'

'Whoa.' Georgia put her hand to her forehead. 'I'm reeling here. You're going to be a single dad?'

'I'm her father. She's my flesh and blood. There is no choice.'

'You're sure Nina is yours?'

'Have I done a DNA test? No time for that yet. But she's mine all right. Looking at her is like looking into a miniature mirror. The social worker from the hospital laughed when she saw me. "No doubt about this little one's daddy," she said.'

Georgia nodded thoughtfully, as he had seen her do so many times. 'That's reassuring. And she must be very cute if she looks like you. But have you really thought this through?'

'She's my child and I will do my duty by her.'

He'd been orphaned at five years old. His

time in foster care had marked him for life. No way in the world would any child of his go through what he had gone through. But he couldn't tell Georgia that. For all the years of their friendship he'd never told her—or anyone from his 'new life' in Sydney—the truth about his childhood back in Melbourne. He'd made no secret that he'd been adopted. But as far as his university friends were concerned he'd been adopted at five by his wonderful parents. Not at fourteen years of age. Not after having found himself in a heap of trouble for doing what he'd thought was the right thing.

'Good for you,' Georgia said. 'But it won't be easy. I guess you know that.'

'None of it will be easy,' he said. 'Which is why I've come here to ask you for your help. I need a friend—' She started to protest but he spoke over her. 'I know I probably don't deserve your friendship, not after those years of radio silence. But I'm asking you anyway, Georgie. For moral support. Please come with me to Katoomba. Today.'

Her eyes widened and she frowned. '*Me? Why?*'

'You know about kids. You teach elementary school. You have nieces and nephews by the bucketload.' He didn't want to sound desperate. But none of his friends had started families yet. Not that he would expect them to put their own lives aside and rush to his help.

Yet he expected that of Georgia. He pushed the uncomfortable thought aside. She had always been there for him. Until he hadn't been there for her. But Nina needed him. And he needed Georgia.

'That doesn't make me an expert on babies,' she said.

'More of an expert than I am,' he said. 'I'd never even held a baby until the social worker handed Nina to me two days ago.' He'd been petrified he'd drop her, despite the social worker's reassurance.

'I'm one ahead of you there,' Georgia said with a wry twist to her mouth. She'd used to tell him she was the 'afterthought' in her family—eight years younger than her youngest sister, ten years younger than her oldest. They were both married with kids. She'd done a lot of babysitting. If anyone knew how to look after a baby, it was her.

'That's why I thought—' he started.

'Don't you have a girlfriend?'

'No.' The relationship with Angie had burned him too badly to even contemplate dating.

'There must be someone else who could—?'

'There's no one else I would trust.'

She sighed, took a step back from him against the stack of boxes in the middle of her living room. Pushed her fingers through her riot of dark chestnut, wavy hair. 'That's not fair, Wil. After all this time you can't just rock up here and—'

'I've been a bad friend, I know,' he said. Wil didn't expect her to disagree and she didn't.

'I… We… Your friends thought you'd dropped us because when you struck it so rich with your inventions, you wanted to leave us behind.' She looked up at him, her eyes huge with undisguised hurt and bewilderment. He hated that he had hurt her.

'That's not how it happened at all,' he said. *How could she have thought that of him?* Yes, he had made a lot of money but it hadn't changed things, hadn't changed *him*. He clenched his hands into fists by his sides. He never wanted Georgia to think badly of him. 'I felt obligated to do what Angie wanted. She was jealous of you. Thought the others looked down at her.'

By the time he had realised Angie had purposely alienated him from the friends he cared most about, it had been impossible to make amends to them.

'That wasn't true,' Georgia said.

But she didn't quite meet his eye. None of

his friends had liked Angie. If only he'd listened to them, instead of being swept along on an ill-founded urge to be some kind of white knight and rescue her from the effects of her troubled past.

'Fact was, Angie didn't like me seeing you. Didn't believe in platonic friendship between a man and a woman. No matter how many times I assured her we were just friends, that we could all be friends. That there was no reason for her to be so jealous.'

'No reason at all to be jealous,' she echoed. 'We rode horses together. Saw indie bands that no one else liked. But there was never any romance.'

'Angie didn't believe me,' he said. Instead she'd screamed awful, ill-founded accusations he had no intention of sharing with Georgia.

'And after your marriage ended? Still no word from you.'

He gritted his teeth. 'I didn't want to admit what a mistake I'd made by marrying her.'

Georgia would never know how many times he'd got as far as the last digit in her phone number before hanging up. How many times he'd driven past this apartment, slowing down only to accelerate away at the thought of confessing what an idiot he'd been to be taken in so thoroughly by Angie. Because to do that would have meant revealing the truth about those hidden years of his life. And not even the comfort and understanding he might have got from his long-standing friend Georgia had been worth that.

'Really,' she muttered. But the icy edge to her voice was melting.

'I'm sorry, Georgie. If I could go back and change things I would.'

She blinked rapidly, something she'd always done when she was thinking deeply about something important. Finally, she spoke. 'I'm not one to hold a grudge. I see things must have been difficult for you. And now—'

'You'll come with me to pick up Nina? That is, if you don't have a boyfriend who has claims on your time.'

'No. There's no one.'

'What about Toby? I thought for sure he'd have a ring on your finger by now.'

'We broke up a year ago,' she said, tight-lipped.

Good. 'I'm sorry,' he said to be polite. He'd been convinced she'd marry Toby. He cursed under his breath. If he'd known Toby was going to exit her life, he mightn't have made that rash decision to marry Angie.

She gestured around her. 'I'm in the middle of moving house. The landlord has put the apartment on the market and I'm going home to my parents' until I find a new place. There are boxes still to pack, cleaning to be done. I—'

'I'll pay for packers, movers and professional cleaners. Please, Georgie.'

She paused, looked up at him with an expression he knew of old, halfway between exasperation and affection, then sighed. 'For past times' sake,' she said. 'No, for the baby's sake. Unless you've changed a lot in the two years since I last saw you, I'm not so sure you'd know which end was up on a seven-month-old baby.' Her smile—that lovely smile that had always uplifted him—danced around the edges of her lips.

Wil didn't realise he'd been holding his breath until he let it out on a *whoosh* of relief.

'Thank you,' he said.

Now that Georgia was back in his life, he wouldn't let her go again too easily. No matter what it took.

CHAPTER TWO

SO MANY TIMES during the years of her friendship with Wil, Georgia had escaped the city with him to head for the Blue Mountains, west of Sydney, to ride horses or bush walk. Only never with a rearward-facing baby car seat installed in the back seat of Wil's car. Or four large packets of disposable nappies stacked next to it. 'Just in case they're all needed on the way home,' Wil explained.

Georgia laughed. 'Unless the baby has a particularly explosive digestive system, I very much doubt that.'

He scowled in a way she well remembered. 'I told you, I know nothing about babies.'

She almost said, *You've got a lot to learn.* But Wil seemed only too aware of that. She almost asked if he was nervous about collecting the baby, but the tight set of his jaw and the way his hands gripped the wheel so his knuckles showed white gave her the answer.

'You'll learn quickly,' she said instead, making it her mission to encourage and support him as she'd always done as his friend. And avoid jokes about dirty nappies. He was facing completely new territory without much of a map to guide him. She fought the urge to reach out and place her hand over his to reassure him, but that had never been the way with them. *No touching.*

'I guess I'll have to,' he said.

Her friend had come back so unexpectedly into her life. She was churning with curiosity about what had happened in the two years since she had seen him. So many questions clamoured to be asked. But now wasn't the time to ask them.

Wil was essentially a very private person. It took time for him to confide in his friends. Things must have ended badly for him to have been so estranged from Angie he hadn't even known she was pregnant. Georgia admired the way he had stepped up to his duty as a father. Not every twenty-eight-year-old guy would react the same way to news of a secret baby. But then she'd always thought of Wil as one of the good guys.

She'd met him at orientation day on the first day of her first year at Sydney University. Thrilled by the newness of it all, she'd signed up for various interest clubs and had been searching for the equestrian club when she'd bumped into a tall, dark-haired guy doing the same thing. One glance had told her he was a country boy, his Western jeans, blue and white checked shirt and elastic-sided riding boots a dead giveaway. All that had been missing was an Akubra, the iconic Australian wide-brimmed hat.

'They've closed the equestrian club for lack of interest,' he'd said gloomily.

'But I'm interested,' she'd said.

'So am I,' he'd said.

'That makes two of us.'

Then they'd looked at each other—really looked—and laughed. 'Why don't we start our own club?' he'd said.

'Let's go grab a coffee and talk about how we'd do that,' she'd said.

Excitement had hummed through her. He had been quite the hottest guy she'd seen on campus. But from the get-go it had been strictly a hands-off scenario. Wil had just started dating a girl and she'd still been seeing her high-school boyfriend. Despite that—per-haps because of that—she and Wil had fallen immediately into an easy friendship, talking non-stop for more than an hour. They'd done nothing about reviving the moribund university equestrian club. But the next weekend they'd driven up together to the Blue Mountains to horseback ride in the Megalong Valley.

This time, their hour-and-a-half journey to the mountains took them to a suburban area on the wrong side of Katoomba. Wil told her that his ex-wife had moved up there after their final split. The streets were steep and hilly, lined with small, free-standing houses, the bush never too far away. Georgia laughed when they had to sound the horn at a small flock of sheep grazing at the side of the road. No dimple from Wil. He was obviously too focused on what was to come to engage in her speculation about whether the sheep had escaped, or it was considered okay up here for sheep to wander all over a suburban street.

He pulled up in front of a shabby but tidy cottage, surrounded by a neat garden. 'This is the sister's place,' he said. 'She's been looking after Nina since the accident.' He made no move to get out of the car.

'Nina is such a pretty name,' she said.

'Yeah. I like it,' he said.

Georgia let him sit there, his gaze focused on the bright blue front door of the house, until the silence got uncomfortable. 'So, *operation baby pick up*,' she prompted. 'What's the next step?'

'The social worker Maree meets us at the house to facilitate the handover. She's in there now.'

'And then you're a daddy,' she said. It scarcely seemed real to her. He would walk out of that house with a baby in his arms. A baby for keeps.

Wil turned to her, the colour drained from his face. 'That's what terrifies me. I want to do the right thing. But what do I know about being a dad? It's not just the nappies or what to feed her. I'll nail that. Suppose I haven't got it in me to be a good parent?'

The anguish in his face told her there was something more going on here. She'd often had the feeling there was more to Wil than he'd ever let on to her. Something, perhaps, to do with his upbringing. She knew he'd been orphaned as a young child. But as a friend she'd never questioned his past. Right now he needed morale-boosting more than anything else.

'The fact that you feel responsible for her is a very good start. That you're actually *here* is a huge point in your favour.'

'Guys usually have time to get used to the idea of being a father.' He drummed his fingers on the edge of the steering wheel. 'I've been thrown in the deep end.'

'That's true. You'll have to learn on the spot. But you're a clever guy. It seems to me that so far you're doing great.'

'She's a baby now, but then she'll be a little girl, then a teenager. I'll be the father of a *teenager*, Georgie. How do I do that?'

'It is a bit hard to imagine, isn't it?' she said. She and Wil had been teenagers when they'd met; it didn't seem that long ago. 'But you'll grow with her and the next thing you know you'll be giving her away at her wedding.'

'Father of the bride? That's a stretch too far,' he said with a hint of that dimple finally appearing.

There was something about his slow smile, the way it lit his dark eyes, that had always made her believe she was special to Wil— *as a friend*. She could only imagine what it might be like to have that smile directed at her in the sensual, exciting way that had had women flocking to him. But she had never allowed herself to imagine it. Too scared that if she ever acted on it he might kindly reject her. She wasn't about to start now.

'Wil, what you're doing will be life-changing. There's no way around that. But take it baby step by baby step,' she said, returning his smile.

'You always know the right thing to say,' he said.

'Not always.' *I'm afraid my give-a-damn quota has expired.* 'But in this case, I say just go in and get your baby. I'll show you how to change a nappy if the need arises. How about that for an act of friendship?'

He grimaced. 'Changing nappies is one aspect of parenthood I'm not looking forward to. Prepared for it but dreading it.'

'Hey, you muck out stables. You'll get used to it.' She certainly hadn't, no matter how much she loved her little nieces and nephews. Maybe nappy-changing would be more bearable if the child was your own. Anyway, Wil could well afford to hire a nanny to help him with the practical aspects of parenting.

'You're right. I'm going in,' he said. He unbuckled his seat belt with a resolute air, as if gearing himself up for action on a battlefield. Four days ago he had had no idea he was a father.

'Do you want me to actually come inside with you?' she asked, trying to sound as if she didn't mind either way. She wasn't sure if he'd just wanted her company on the drive. Of course she was dying of curiosity to see what the baby was like, but mainly she wanted to be there for him—someone on his side.

He turned to her. 'Please. I don't know that I can do this without your support.'

'Of course you could.' She undid her seat belt. 'But there's strength in numbers and I'm very happy to be your wing woman.'

A drier heat than humid Sydney, crisp with the sharp scent of eucalypts from the thousands of acres of national park that surrounded the mountain town. The sound of cicadas serenading summer was almost deafening. She stood with Wil at the top of the driveway to the sister's house and smoothed down the skirt of her grape-coloured linen shift dress. Teamed with a low-heeled court shoe, it was a favourite schoolteacher outfit, smart yet respectable. Just the thing to help her friend claim his child.

'I want to do this,' he said fiercely. 'I'll fight to have this child with me. *She's mine.*'

'I've never seen anyone more fearless on horseback. You can do it. You really can, Wil.'

She didn't want to admit she was nervous. This was so out of her experience, had happened so quickly. One minute she'd been packing boxes, just hours later she was in the mountains with Wil, whom she hadn't seen for two years, to pick up his baby. The baby he hadn't known existed. It seemed surreal to say the least.

He turned to look down into her face, dark

eyes sincere and warm with gratitude. *It was so good to be with him again.* 'Thank you,' he said slowly. 'I'll owe you one after this.'

'You don't owe me a thing,' she said. 'I'm happy to help. No exchange of favours required.'

Who knew when she would actually see him again after this? He needed her today, what of tomorrow? Besides, New Wil could be very different from the Old Wil who'd been her friend. Now he was a single dad who'd gone through a nasty divorce and the death of the mother of his child. His life would now be focused totally on a seven-month-old baby. She doubted there would be a lot of time for going to see indie bands, or sharing a meal at a funky city café. There was a real likelihood it might be another two years until she saw him again.

She followed Wil down the pathway. Immediately the sister, Sharyn, opened the door. Georgia saw the resemblance to Angie. The older sister's eyes were red-rimmed, her expression truculent as she glared first at Wil and then at her. The middle-aged social worker hovered nearby.

'I'm so sorry for your loss,' Georgia murmured to Sharyn. 'I knew Angie.' It wasn't simply the polite thing to say, she meant every word. The shocking loss of a young woman, a mother, was genuine cause for sorrow and grief, no matter how she'd felt about her.

'Another loss to come,' Sharyn muttered, still glaring at Wil, who was scrupulously polite in the face of such obvious hostility.

The social worker, Maree, defused the situation and Georgia followed Wil into the house. Small shoes lined up in the entranceway, a stroller leaned against the wall, parked so they had to walk around it, tiny raincoats slung over a rack. A multi-child household. Georgia recognised the signs from her sisters' houses.

The social worker ushered her and Wil into a family room, clean and tidy save for the toys scattered on the floor. A large playpen, of the old-fashioned wooden kind, was set up in the middle of the room.

'Sharyn tells me little Nina just woke up from her nap, and is playing with her cousins,' the social worker said, indicating the playpen.

Georgia's gaze was drawn to the baby with a shock of dark hair and wearing a pink cotton romper suit. She sat on her bottom on a rug, opposite a little boy of about six who waved a fluffy toy rabbit in front of her. Another younger boy stood outside the playpen hanging on to the railing, calling encouragement. The baby laughed, an infectious gurgling kind of laugh that showed four tiny teeth, two top and two bottom. She waved her little arms around in delight as she made a lunge for the toy. Georgia smiled, a smile that came all the way from her heart.

Wil's daughter. Angie's child too. Little Nina had the best of both of them. Wil's dark hair and eyes; Angie's petite nose and heart-shaped face. Georgia's heart spasmed. Poor little thing to have lost her mother. Poor Angie, to have lived long enough after the accident to know she wouldn't survive to see her baby grow up. But Nina had a good man for a father. She'd won the genetic lottery there.

'She's adorable,' Georgia murmured as she looked up to Wil, standing beside her.

At first, she didn't know if he actually heard her. He was staring, transfixed, at his daughter. Emotions rippled across his face. Trepidation. Awe. A warmth that looked very much like pride. *A Wil she'd never seen before.*

'Yes, she is,' he said softly, his eyes not leaving the baby.

Sharyn approached the playpen, breaking the moment like a rock thrown violently into the gentle ripples of a pool. 'Okay, Kieran, that's enough playtime. Give Nina the bunny and take your brother outside to play.'

The boys obeyed without question. Georgia's schoolteacher eye noted both little boys looked well cared for, in the way of children who were active and well nourished. They were tender and gentle with the baby. The older one gave his tiny cousin a kiss, hopped out of the playpen, took his little brother by the hand, and headed out of a sliding door to a grassed area outside.

Little Nina had turned at the sound of her aunt's voice. Now she put up her arms to be picked up. Sharyn immediately swept her into her arms with a murmured endearment. She stood facing Wil. 'You're still determined to take her?' she said. The baby rested comfortably on her hip.

'She's my daughter, Sharyn,' he said. 'We've gone through all this.' Georgia could see a pulse throbbing at his temple that belied the calmness of his voice.

'You didn't even know you had a daughter,' Sharyn said. 'Angie hated you. Wanted to punish you by keeping Nina from you.'

Maree the social worker placed herself between Sharyn and Wil. 'We've discussed this. Legal aspects aside, your sister's dying wish was very clear. She wanted Nina to be in the custody of her father, Wil. I can understand your sadness at little Nina going but—'

'Rightly or wrongly, all Angie would have been thinking of was Wil's money and Nina having access to it,' said Sharyn. 'I told her that Nina should know her father but Angie wanted revenge on her ex for kicking her out. She wanted her secret kept until one day she could taunt him about Nina and blackmail him for more money in return for seeing his little girl.'

Georgia shuddered at the matter-of-fact tone of Sharyn's voice as she discussed her sister's warped motivation. Wil's expression didn't change but the words must have hurt. 'That changes nothing,' he said.

Sharyn hugged the baby closer to her. 'Nina is happy here with us. I looked after her when her mother was at work. What makes you think you can look after a little girl?' Georgia sensed the pain underneath the anger.

'She's my daughter and belongs with me,' Wil repeated. 'I can look after her very well.'

With Wil's wealth he could give his daughter every advantage. So much more than the aunt could provide. Georgia appreciated that he didn't rub in their difference in social status and income. Besides, she didn't think that was what Wil meant—he meant the special love of a parent, the closest bond a child could have. Father trumped aunt. Wealthy father with doting grandparents, no doubt waiting in the wings, held all the cards.

'You? A guy on your own? A guy who couldn't stay married for even six months?'

Georgia cringed at Wil's sharp intake of breath. 'Yes,' he said, obviously through gritted teeth.

'It's not right.' Sharyn clutched the baby tighter, as if daring Wil to prise her out of her arms. 'If you cared about her, you'd leave her with me. A little girl needs a mother...a woman in her life.'

'She will have a woman in her life,' said Wil. He moved closer to Georgia and put his arm around her. That was the first shock. Then came the second. 'Georgia is my fiancée.'

What?

Georgia stiffened, went to protest. But Wil tightened his grip on her shoulder. She knew what he meant. *Play along.* Back in the day they'd sometimes pretended to be dating to deter an unwanted admirer at a party or out at a bar. Each other's wing person. They'd have a good laugh about it afterwards.

Georgia didn't feel like laughing now. 'Uh, yes.' She forced a smile. *This wasn't a game.*

'Congratulations on your engagement,' said the social worker, looking very pleased.

'Th-thank you,' said Georgia, not able to meet her eye, furious with Wil for putting her on the spot.

'She's an elementary schoolteacher and knows all about little kids,' Wil added. He squeezed Georgia's shoulder again in an unmistakable prompt.

'Uh…yes, I do,' she said. 'And babies. I have five nieces and nephews and have looked after them all. Ask me anything you want about babies.'

Sharyn looked her up and down as if she were something loathsome. 'Angie told me all about *Georgia*. The *best friend* she thought her husband fancied. Looks like she was right not to trust you, if you're now engaged.'

Georgia gasped at the accusation. Went to deny it. Bit her tongue. *This wasn't real.* She was, in truth, just his friend. She had nothing to feel guilty about.

'Not true, Sharyn,' Wil said. 'Georgia was indeed just a friend then.'

Irrationally—because that was all true—his dismissal of her as a woman his wife had had no cause to fear hurt. Georgia schooled herself not to betray just how much it hurt. She'd never tried to be more than *just a friend*, she reminded herself.

Georgia was aware of the woman's narrowed glance at her empty ring finger and she fisted her left hand in response and put it behind her back. Of course people would expect an engagement ring. Guess Wil hadn't thought of that with his spur-of-the-moment comment. Unless he'd planned to say she was his fiancée all along?

She put that thought aside to consider later. By not denying his from-out-of-nowhere claim—how could she have?—she had committed to playing along. Especially as Wil's former sister-in-law seemed still determined to fight.

Wil pulled her closer. She tried to relax against him, difficult when she was so intensely aware of his strength and warmth, the utter masculinity of him. *He still smelled the same.* She'd always managed to deny how attractive she found him. Pretending to be his wife-to-be took her denial to a whole new level.

Sharyn continued. 'But that doesn't qualify you to be a mum. Especially to a little girl who has lost her own. She looks cheerful enough now but she knows her mummy is gone, that something is very wrong in her world.' She choked up but scowled at Georgia's look of sympathy.

Georgia glanced up at Wil, trying to seem like a concerned fiancée seeking reassurance, then back to Sharyn. 'I'll do my best. I should imagine Nina would be a very easy child to…

to love. Just because Nina is going to live with
her dad and…uh…me, doesn't mean she has
to say goodbye for ever to her aunty and cousins. I'm sure Wil will want you to be part of
her life.'

Georgia sensed Wil still beside her. Had she
overstepped the mark, gone where a pretend
fiancée shouldn't go?

'Really?' said Sharyn, relief softening her
combative expression. 'We'll get to see her?'

Georgia was so disconcerted at the situation
she found herself in, she struggled to sound
normal. 'Of course. Family is important.' She
looked back up at him. 'Isn't it, Wil?'

'Yes, it is,' he said with a vehemence that
surprised her.

'So I don't have to tell the boys they'll never
see their baby cousin again?' Sharyn said.

'No. Uh…in fact they could be pageboys at
our wedding.' Georgia had to suppress a grin
at the look on Wil's face. Served him right for
dropping her into this. 'They'd make cute little ring-bearers, wouldn't they, Wil?' she said,
perhaps a little too sweetly.

'Uh, yes,' he muttered.

Sharyn's face lightened. 'Pageboys? I'm
not sure they'd stay still long enough for that,'
she said. 'But you're serious about keeping in
touch?'

Georgia gritted her teeth. How could she possibly be expected to answer such a question? She pasted on a fake fiancée smile as she gave Wil a glance she hoped he would recognise as *over to you.*

'I'll make sure Nina keeps in touch with her cousins,' he said.

His former sister-in-law nodded and reluctantly handed her little niece over to her father. 'Make sure you do,' she said.

Wil took Nina from her, a little awkwardly but with growing confidence. Georgia caught her breath as she watched him.

There was something about a tall, broad-shouldered, manly guy holding a little baby in strong, protective arms that was heart-stoppingly appealing. Even more appealing when the guy in question was her friend Wil, and the little daughter he had only just discovered. He so big and powerful; Nina so small and vulnerable. The way he held her, the intensity of his gaze were as if he was silently assuring Nina he would protect her from every possible bad arrow the world might have in wait for her. But the way the tiny girl looked back up at him with the same dark eyes made Georgia's heart turn over. There was a connection there. Now she really believed it—Wil was a father.

A wave of yearning swept over her. Not

for Wil—of course not for Wil. He was just a *friend*. Or for his daughter. Her days were filled with looking after other women's children. She wanted her own baby one day. At twenty-seven going on twenty-eight, her biological clock had started to tick insistently. But as her track record with marriageable-type males was abysmal, that particular dream might not be coming true any time soon.

She'd knocked back three proposals, the first while she'd still been at uni. Commitment was what she'd craved but the guys just hadn't been quite right. The most recent had been Toby. She'd let the relationship go on for too long, wasting her time and his. But she'd thought that pathway was expected of her— marriage to the steady kind of guy everyone had liked. Children to follow. Even to the fact that Toby had been a fellow schoolteacher— just think how convenient all those school holidays would have been when it came to vacation childcare. But that hadn't been enough for her to want a ring on her finger. Even after Wil had married and dashed any deeply suppressed hope she'd had of their friendship developing into something deeper.

Wil turned to her and smiled. The dimple was in full force. 'Do you want to hold her?' he said, as if offering a gift of inestimable value.

Hold baby Nina? As a potential stepmother? Of course she wanted to hold the dear little thing. But she wasn't sure what Wil expected of her. To gush that she couldn't wait to be little Nina's mummy? That would be going too far in this crazy charade he had thrust her into. She wouldn't—couldn't—lie. Instead, she would try to behave as she normally would when offered a cuddle of an adorable baby.

She held out her arms with a smile, was rewarded with the deliciousness of a soft, sweet-smelling baby in her arms. 'Hello, Nina,' she murmured. 'I'm Georgia.' The baby replied with her cute, four-toothed smile and a string of babble that just might have meant *pleased to meet you*. Nina was, without a doubt, enchanting.

But how dare Wil put her in a position when she had to pretend to be a doting mum-to-be? Engaged to be married to him? It stretched the boundaries of a newly ignited friendship a step too far. She didn't want to fall back into the *good old Georgia* trap—always obliging, always helpful, making excuses for the inexcusable—not for her family, not for her friends and especially not for Wil, who had ignored her for two whole years.

CHAPTER THREE

WIL RISKED A sideways glance at Georgia where she sat next to him in the car as he drove back towards Sydney. Her eyes were closed, but he knew she wasn't asleep.

In two years, she hadn't changed a lot. Her hair, glinting reddish highlights in the afternoon sunlight, was cut a little shorter into a more sophisticated style. Her cheekbones seemed more pronounced and made her look more grown up, more womanly, though the scatter of freckles across the bridge of her nose was still delightfully girlish. She must have had her ears pierced as she was wearing stud earrings he'd never noticed before—she'd never worn earrings for fear of them getting caught in her horse-riding helmet. But she was still riding horses if her toned arms—bare in her sleeveless dress—were any indication.

He was struck again, as he had been many times since they'd reconnected, by how lovely she was. Not in an obvious *look at me* way, but in a quieter way that needed a second glance to be truly appreciated. He'd appreciated her beauty from the get-go, even more so as he'd got to know her. But it wasn't just a tumble of dark hair, deep blue eyes and an oval-shaped face that made her so attractive, it was her warm, generous heart, ready laughter and her smile. Georgia smiled not just with her lips but with her eyes, her whole face lighting up and warming those who were lucky enough to be on the receiving end.

There had been years in Wil's life where smiles bestowed on him had been rare. When he'd first met Georgia, back during his first days of university, her smile had been like a gift. She'd been as disappointed as he had about the lack of an equestrian club, but her good humour about it had soon had him planning how he could continue to see her. Fortunately, riding horses had been an immediate shared interest. He'd had to be convinced by the quirky indie music she favoured but he'd gone along with it as an excuse to see her. Then he'd got to genuinely like it. And to like her. A lot.

He hadn't straight away relegated her to the 'just friends' zone. Far from it. He would have asked her out like a shot that first day at uni if each of them hadn't already been dating other people. As neither of them were the types to cheat, it hadn't happened. Turned out the opportunities where they'd both been single and available at the same time had been rare. But there had been undeniable moments when neither of them had followed up on the chance to step up their friendship to something else. Then he'd got to thinking she was way too valuable as a friend to risk losing her friendship. Yet. Maybe one day he'd take that chance. It had seemed to him that Georgia had 'commitment' stamped all over her. He hadn't been ready for 'for ever'. Girlfriends had come and gone. Georgia had stayed. Until the big mistake that had been his marriage.

Now Georgia was annoyed with him. The tight set of her mouth, the uneven breathing told him she was seething while she pretended to sleep. He knew why.

He should have consulted her before introducing her as his fiancée. But it had been a spur-of-the-moment decision. A gut response to the criticism that he wasn't capable of looking after a baby. Fear that, despite the baby being legally in his custody, somehow the sister and the social worker would block him from taking his daughter home with him.

Georgia had been shocked when he'd made

the outrageous claim, though she'd hidden it well. The rigid way she'd held her shoulders had told him she was less than pleased. Yet she'd stepped up to the plate. She'd made the perfect pretend fiancée. Things wouldn't have gone as smoothly without her intervention. He could never thank her enough.

From the back seat, where baby Nina was strapped into her brand-new baby car seat, came a sudden loud murmur. Georgia's eyes shot open. 'Is Nina okay?' She twisted around to check on her. 'She's still snoozing. Must have been dreaming.'

'I wonder what a seven-month-old baby dreams about?' he said.

'Who knows?' she said. 'Food? Comfort? A former life, perhaps, if you believe in that.'

'Whatever that dream might have been, she sounded happy,' he said with relief.

'She seems a happy baby. Healthy and well cared for too. Angie must have been a good mum.' Georgia's tone was guarded.

Wil knew what his friend had thought of his ex-wife. With good reason, as it had turned out. Angie had made manipulation into an art form. But he'd been so intent on seeing in her an echo of someone from his past, a chance to right a long-ago wrong, he'd been blind to the reality of Angie. He'd cut his losses as soon as he could, paid her what she'd wanted. Hadn't seen her again after she'd moved to Katoomba. Married and separated within six months—not a great track record. Not something he was proud of. Not a mistake he intended to repeat any time soon.

'According to Sharyn, Angie was a good mother,' he said. 'Sharyn told me that when Angie discovered she was pregnant, she reformed her party-girl lifestyle and looked after her health.'

Georgia sighed. 'What a tragedy. Lucky for Nina she's got you.'

'I want to give her everything,' he said fiercely. *Everything I never had.*

Georgia fell silent as they started the descent from the Upper Mountains. The Great Western Highway twisted through charming small townships that Sydneysiders liked to visit for the autumn colour, the winter chill, to enjoy the distinct seasons that didn't really apply to subtropical Sydney. Much of the road was through bushland with eucalypt forest growing right to the edge. In the summer heat, he was aware of the sharp tang of the gum leaves, the faint chime of the bellbirds.

When he stopped at a traffic light, Georgia turned to him. She was flushed high on her cheekbones. The words that had obviously been brewing spilled out. 'Why? Why the fake fiancée thing? Why put me on the spot like that?'

Wil wished he could tell her the real reasons. Unload some of the burden of his past. Confess how he distrusted social workers. His dread of leaving a child—any child—in the care of an aunt. That his fears had festered since he was a five-year-old, orphaned and left in the reluctant custody of his father's sister, who had kept him out of a grudging sense of duty and absolutely no love. He'd run away. More than once. The last time had delivered him into the welfare system. Many social workers had followed, some better than others, all overworked and not inclined to spend more time than necessary with a boy labelled as trouble. But the masks he'd been forced to wear for all those years for self-protection were too firmly in place to risk letting Georgia see behind them.

'You heard Sharyn's scorn at the idea of me looking after a baby. *A man.* As if I wasn't capable.' His former sister-in-law's words had triggered his own deep-seated fears about the sudden fatherhood that had been thrust upon him. He'd fought back with his best defence— Georgia.

'She didn't think too much of me looking after a baby, either,' said Georgia with a strangled laugh. 'In spite of you trumpeting my extensive childcare experience.'

'Sharyn was out of order. I'm sorry you were exposed to her attack,' he said, grateful that the light changed to green and he didn't have to directly face her.

'She was grieving. I didn't take offence. In a way she was right. Looking after other people's children must be very different from caring for your own, with day-in, day-out responsibility.'

As he was about to find out. 'Point taken. But I didn't want to argue with her. Or the social worker, who'd whip a child into care sooner than not if they had any doubt about the parent's capacity.'

Georgia tilted her head questioningly. 'What makes you say that? I thought she was supportive of you. It's a social worker's priority to keep children with their parents.'

Wil sensed Georgia's frown, the unasked questions about his childhood. All he'd ever told her was that he'd been adopted, lived with his adoptive parents and their birth son on a historic rural property raising cattle and growing wheat in south-western Victoria. He'd gone to boarding school in Melbourne and then university in Sydney. A seemingly idyllic, privileged life. The years between five and thirteen, in and out of foster homes and children's institutions, were the blanks in his history he had no intention of filling in. Not for Georgia, not for anyone if he could avoid it.

'But did you note Maree's relief when she heard I had a fiancée?' he said.

He knew Georgia rolled her eyes even without having to see her. 'Which of course you don't. The social worker might have believed your fabrication. Sharyn sussed out something was fishy because I wasn't wearing an engagement ring. I hope this deception doesn't come back to bite you. Or me, for that matter.'

'How could it? The "deception" won't go further than today. It was a temporary ruse. When I see Sharyn again, I'll just tell her it didn't work out for us.'

'As easy as that,' Georgia said too lightly.

He cursed himself for his thoughtlessness. She'd been such a good sport about all this. 'I didn't mean our friendship. I meant—'

'I know what you meant,' she said drily.

She had been so calm, so unflustered, rising to the challenge of playing a fake fiancée beyond even his expectations. As far as friends went, Georgia was the gold standard.

'Thank you,' he said. 'You're being very gracious about it.'

'I'm not, actually. I'm cranky as hell. Not

with Sharyn. With *you*. She was fighting for a child she loves, her last link with her sister. You took advantage of me, threw me into the situation totally unprepared. We've only just re-established contact with each other. You went too far, Wil. It was a crazy thing to do.'

'It wasn't premeditated, I assure you. But I can't regret my strategy, not for a moment. You were brilliant. I'm so grateful to you for going along with me.' Thank heaven he'd found the guts to call on her that morning.

Georgia frowned. 'I still don't get why you did it. Surely introducing me as a good female friend would have been enough?'

'A fiancée sounds more stable. These government people are looking for stability and continuity.'

'Why should you worry? It wasn't an adoption. You're the father. Her closest blood relative. Your name is on the birth certificate. Nina's mother's dying wish was that you have custody. Sharyn doesn't have any rights.'

Wil simply didn't trust the system, not when he'd been a victim of it in the past. Perhaps it had changed since he'd been a ward of the state, perhaps not. But his memories of his experience of the welfare system would always be raw. 'I wasn't going to allow anything—or anyone—to get in the way of me claiming my daughter. Bringing you into the picture was a good way to get Sharyn off my back.'

'Actually, I didn't think Sharyn was that bad either. She obviously cares for Nina in her own way.'

Of course Georgia would try to be fair. Her determination to see the good in people was something he'd always liked about her. He didn't refer to her comment about the page-boys. When she'd made the teasing remark, a sudden image had flashed through his mind of Georgia walking up a church aisle, radiantly beautiful in a white wedding dress, with Sharyn's two little boys walking earnestly ahead of her balancing wedding rings on satin cushions. Where the hell had that come from? It wasn't something he wanted to revisit, that was for sure.

'Were you serious about maintaining a relationship with Nina's aunt and cousins?' she said. 'Or was that another expedient lie to help you get what you wanted?' Georgia had always been quick to the point.

'Not a lie. Those little boys seemed like good kids.' As, perhaps, he had been before his young life had shattered into pieces around him.

'It would be good for your little girl to grow up knowing her cousins. I loved my boy cousins, though at times they seemed like a different breed.'

'That's why I agreed to it. I don't care much for Sharyn. But it's all about Nina. What's good for her. That's all that concerns me now. Whatever she needs I will make sure she gets. If it's extended family, I'll go along with it for her sake.'

Wil recognised that from now on his own needs would come a very poor second to the tiny person asleep in the back of the car. His life would never be the same. He needed Georgia. He had to make sure she stuck around. As his friend. As Nina's friend. He couldn't lose her again.

What next? As they finished their descent from the mountains and joined the motorway that would take them back into Sydney, Georgia wondered—not for the first time—if Wil had fully thought this single-fatherhood thing through.

'Do you really not know how to change a nappy?' she asked.

'What single guy my age would know about nappies? But I've read the instructions on the packet. It doesn't look too difficult. The woman in the pharmacy where I bought them gave me a demonstration.'

Georgia tried to smother her laugh but without success.

'So you think it's funny too?' he said, that scowl back in force. 'The pharmacy lady seemed to think it was highly amusing.'

With his dark brows and eyes, Wil had always managed an impressive scowl. Georgia put up her hands, as if to ward him off. 'I'm not saying anything,' she said, mirth still bubbling through her words.

'No. But you're still laughing,' he said. 'I also watched some online videos. Nappy-changing tutorials. How to bathe a baby. That kind of thing. And I signed up to follow some mommy bloggers. They seem to know everything. It's all there if you know where to look.'

'What's all there, Wil?' she asked. She found the idea of handsome, clever Wil earnestly watching childcare videos more than a tad endearing.

'How to be a parent,' he said very seriously. 'The practical stuff, anyway.'

'Okay,' she said cautiously.

'And Sharyn gave me a comprehensive list of Nina's likes and dislikes. Even packed that toy rabbit she loves into her bag.'

'Sounds like you're all sorted, then,' Georgia said, biting her tongue. And reminding herself again that he could afford an around-the-clock nanny. She wasn't going to jump in doing her *good old Georgia* thing again, always first with the offer of help.

She was over being taken for granted by anyone. Her people-pleasing had always been part of her. Perhaps because of being born the 'accidental' third child, whose unexpected arrival had interrupted her mother's career and disrupted the family dynamics, she'd been so amenable to try and earn her place.

Until recently she'd kept it up, house-sitting, cat-sitting, babysitting for her family—even when inconvenient, even when she'd resented their assumption that she would always be on call. She'd overdone it with Toby, being too compliant, perhaps to make up for her instinct that she didn't love him enough. She'd been super sweet to his overbearing parents. Had spent weekends, where she'd rather have been horse riding, cheering him on in the rugby games she'd found tedious beyond belief because he'd liked her to be there.

Looking back on her friendship with Wil, trying to puzzle why he'd ghosted her, she'd realised the caring and sharing element had been unbalanced there too. To a certain extent, she'd been there for him to pick up and put down when he'd pleased. When she'd ended it with Toby, she'd decided to put herself first for a change. Follow her own interests. And it was working out great. Now Wil was back in the picture and she'd have to stick to her resolve—no more being a doormat for anyone.

'Where are you actually living these days? Still in Pyrmont?' she asked. She shuddered at the thought of a baby learning to walk in his harbour-side penthouse with balconies on two sides and hard, shiny surfaces everywhere.

'I kept the apartment as an investment and bought a property in Ingleside after my marriage broke up.'

'Wow. I'm envious.' Ingleside was a suburb on Sydney's northern beaches, close to both bushland and sea. Once home to market gardeners, now known for large plots of land with big houses and priced way out of the regular wage-earner's reach. But not, it seemed, her wealthy friend Wil's. 'Is there room for horses?'

'You betcha. I have two stabled there for me to ride. An Arab gelding and a thoroughbred mare.'

'Country boy in the city,' she said. 'Lucky you.' She wanted to ask could she come down and see them, beg for a ride on one of the horses, but she wasn't sure what shape her friendship with New Wil, single dad Wil, might take.

'It's a big house, a big garden,' he said. 'I didn't know about Nina when I bought it, but it will be a great place for her to grow up.'

'She's a lucky girl to have you as her dad. And not just because, no doubt, she'll have her own pony.'

'Starting with a miniature as soon as she's big enough to mount one,' he said.

'But that's a while off. What preparations have you made for her now? Babies seem to need a lot of stuff.' She wasn't as confident as he seemed to be on the value of online tutorials. Yet she didn't want to undermine his confidence in his parenting skills.

'All sorted,' he said. 'The day after I got back from my first trip to Katoomba I visited one of those big baby stores. A very helpful girl helped me get everything I needed and it was delivered the next day.'

There would, no doubt, be many very helpful girls extending a hand to this handsome, wealthy single dad and his cute baby. He'd be bowled over with offers of help once the news got out. His care for his daughter only made him more attractive.

Despite her annoyance at him about the fake-fiancée fiasco, she was glad she'd been there for him today. It was a privilege to have been present to witness the moment he'd first taken charge of his daughter—an emotional, significant occasion. She wished… *No.* She didn't want to become more involved. She was as vulnerable as anyone else to the appeal of this gorgeous man with his adorable little girl. *Just friends*, she reminded herself for, quite possibly, the millionth time since she'd met him.

'Have you been able to get a good nanny at this short notice?' she asked.

'There won't be any nanny. I told you, I'm going to look after my baby myself. I need to bond with her. Not leave her with strangers.'

'Okay,' she said. She admired him for his conviction. Didn't want to make any comment that might be construed as sexist. 'What about your work? How will you manage both working and being a stay-at-home dad?' Her sisters seemed to be endlessly juggling.

'These days I run a design and engineering solutions consultancy. My staff are mainly freelance. I intend to shift my centre of operations to a home office. I've had to think on the spot. Fortunately, January is our quiet time.'

'You seem to have it sorted,' she said.

'It will be more a work in progress. I just want to do my best for my daughter.'

'Keep in touch, won't you?' She didn't want

to go back to friend limbo with Wil. Not after this dramatic reconciliation. 'I'll be wondering how you and Nina will be managing.'

'I'm sure we'll be fine,' he said, with typical Wil confidence.

'The entire Internet is on standby to give assistance,' she said lightly.

Not to mention all the other resources available to a millionaire. Those resources would not include her. *Good old Georgia*, always on hand, had gone on strike. She'd told her sisters to count her out for free babysitting all summer. She had a life of her own and at age twenty-seven she darn well wanted to develop it.

'When I drop you back at your apartment, give me all the details I need to organise the movers for you,' he said.

'That won't be necessary, I—'

'No arguments,' he said. 'It's the least I can do for your help today.'

'Okay, I won't argue,' she said. In truth, his offer was more than welcome. She'd be packing all night otherwise.

'How long do you plan to stay at your parents' place?'

'Long enough to sort out where I really want to live. I want to go to Greece in the July school vacation. Then I'm thinking of maybe getting a transfer to a rural school. I don't know that I'll ever be able to afford to buy my own place in Sydney.'

'You're really planning to leave Sydney?' Wil sounded shocked.

'Maybe. One day. It's an option. That's a good thing about teaching. There are jobs in the country. The other good thing is the holidays, of course.'

'Have you got the rest of this summer vacation off?'

'All of January.'

'Are you going away?' He still seemed disconcerted at the revelation she might be leaving Sydney. Did he think she'd put her life on hold these past two years? That now he'd got back in touch she'd be always on tap?

She shook her head. 'I have to work. Well, I don't know that I can really call it something as onerous as work when it's a dream come true for me.'

'Something to do with your art?' *He remembered.*

'I got a publishing contract. A children's picture book. I wrote and illustrated it.' Excitement and disbelief bubbled through her voice; she still could hardly believe it was true. But it hadn't happened until she'd made her own interests her priority.

'Congratulations,' he said, sounding genuinely pleased for her. 'I always knew you were talented. Well done.'

'My first book comes out in March. My next deadline is February. That will keep me very busy over the holidays.'

'My friend the author,' he said slowly. 'I like the sound of that.'

'Not as much as I like it,' she said, laughing.

'You'll be busy. But if you could find time to visit me and Nina, I'd like that.'

'Me too, Wil,' she said.

Her heart gave a skip of pleasure at the thought. Wil back in her life. She didn't want to get too involved. His ghosting of her still stung, and she wasn't convinced he wouldn't do it again. Then there was the way he'd dropped her into the pretend engagement without any consultation. But they had a lot of catching up to do. She ached to know more about what he'd been doing. Of course the presence of a third little person would change the dynamics. But she could see no reason why she and Wil couldn't ditch the fake-fiancée thing for good and pick up their friendship again. On her terms.

CHAPTER FOUR

WHAT THE HECK was she doing back in what had been her childhood bedroom at age twenty-seven—turning twenty-eight next month? Georgia finished stuffing her carefully curated selection of clothes into the three skinny drawers her parents had allocated for her use; the rest of her stuff was in storage. When she'd left home, they'd turned her old room into a study for her mother. All traces of her occupancy were long gone, but there was a disturbing sense of déjà vu about it. Under the coat of tasteful dove-grey paint that covered the acid yellow she had favoured for her bedroom, she swore she could still detect the shadows of her horse posters taped to the wall.

It was ironic, because the room had actually started off as a study. It had become a bedroom for Georgia when she'd been born eight years after the youngest of her two older sisters. Their 'happy accident', her parents had called her, but she'd always felt they'd tacked on the 'happy' in an effort to make her feel better about it. She'd been their disappointment too. After two daughters, they'd hoped their 'afterthought'—she'd also had to live with that label—would be a longed-for son. They'd been saving her great-grandfather's name of George for his birth. But they'd got Georgia instead.

She sometimes wondered if that was why she'd turned out such a tomboy, happier in jeans and riding boots than the girly dresses her sisters loved. Perhaps trying to live up to the name they'd really wanted.

It wasn't that she hadn't been loved. Her parents were wonderful, her mother a lawyer, her father a university professor. She had good relationships with her sisters too, even if they did have a tendency to think they knew what was best for her. Sometimes she'd felt she'd had four parents expecting her to fall into line, needing to please. To their credit, her family had taken her new stance on not being as available to help out as she'd always been with good grace, if not without some good-natured teasing.

Georgia placed the last folded T-shirt in the over-stuffed drawer, along with her mother's staples and sticky tape, sliding it carefully shut.

It had come as a shock when the landlord had given her notice on the North Sydney apartment, but in a way it had been a kick-in-the-butt blessing. Her life had been on hold for the last year since the split with Toby. Same flatmates. Same job. There were places she longed to see, stories she ached to tell, new experiences to embrace. Now was her chance to pole-vault out of the rut her life had become as she headed towards thirty. She had stopped being such a people-pleaser but she had to take control of the direction her future would take. And that included not rushing into any long-term leases on apartments.

When Wil's ID flashed up on her mobile phone she looked at it for a long moment before picking up. Two years since she'd been used to seeing calls from Wil. She still wasn't sure what she thought about his sudden reappearance. How to handle her mixed feelings about a rekindling of their friendship. 'I was just about to call to thank you for the professional movers you arranged for yesterday,' she said. 'They got me all packed up and moved without any fuss.'

'Glad that worked out,' he said. 'It was the least I could do for disrupting your day.'

'I appreciated it,' she said. She was still a little cranky with him over the fake-fiancée thing. The more she'd thought about it, the more she'd realised how out of order he'd been to spring that on her. 'How's Nina? And you, of course. Transition to fatherhood going well?'

'It's okay,' he said. But it wasn't. Even without seeing him, she could tell he was on edge. The old connection between them was still there.

'Is it really okay?'

There was a deep intake of breath. 'I could do with some help.'

Why was she not surprised? Help from good old Georgia required, no doubt. 'Is that Nina I hear wailing in the background?' she asked.

'I can't get her to settle.' She could sense a quiet note of desperation in Wil's voice, usually so confident and self-assured. 'She's been howling like that for more than an hour.'

'Have you fed her?'

'Yes.'

'Same food Sharyn was giving her?'

'I followed instructions precisely.'

'Changed her?'

'Yes. I'm getting the hang of it. That sticky tab system could do with some improvement, though.' Georgia smiled to herself at that. Nothing like a challenge to Wil's fix-it soul.

'Cuddled her?'

'Who knew I could rustle up the words to "Rock-a-bye Baby"?'

The thought of Wil rocking his sweet little daughter in his strong, muscular arms and singing to her sent a spasm to her heart. This was definitely a New Wil. But should she be so surprised? He'd always been scrupulous in his care of the horses he rode, kind and affectionate towards them. Not all riders were. He'd always been kind to her too. Until he'd so brutally terminated their friendship.

'But nothing is working?' she asked.

'The struggle is real. She was fine yesterday. I don't know what's the matter with her today.'

Georgia didn't have the heart to suggest baby Nina could be missing her mother, her aunt and everything familiar in her young life.

She dredged her memory for any other strategies her sisters used to calm a crying baby. 'Have you tried popping Nina in her car seat and driving around the block? That can work.'

'I hadn't thought of that but I'm prepared to try anything.' He paused. 'Georgie, could you—?'

'Come down to your house?' So much for being on strike. But this was a baby in distress. And possibly a dad in distress. It would be heartless to stand on principle. 'Now?' The wailing in the background got louder and angrier.

'Please.'

'Shall I pick up something for lunch on the way?' She'd been just about to make a sandwich.

'No. There's plenty of food. Just get here.'

'I'm at my parents' place in Lindfield. Give me thirty minutes.'

'Be quick. I really need you.'

Until the next Angie came along?

Georgia put a tight rein on her urge to say she'd do anything she could to help. Seeing him again had brought the pain he had caused her rushing back. His sudden severing of their friendship had hurt as much as any relationship break-up. More. She wouldn't risk that kind of pain again too easily. She had to be careful to keep her distance from Wil's domestic dilemmas. This would be just the one time she rushed to his help.

Forty minutes later—even with satellite she'd got a bit lost—Georgia drove along a narrow road lined with bushland to reach Wil's house in Ingleside. She pulled up at the address he'd texted her. Then sat there, gaping.

This was Wil's house? High sandstone walls formed a boundary on either side of wide wrought-iron gates. Through the gates, she could see a long gravel driveway that ran up to the house, an imposing colonial-style building with sandstone foundations and wide verandas on three sides. The house was framed by palm trees and surrounded by lush gardens, the centrepiece of which was a three-tiered fountain that splashed and sparkled in the midday sun.

For just the teensiest moment, she felt intimidated, as if her small white hatchback, a gift from her parents on her twenty-first birthday, didn't belong among such opulence. Her parents were reasonably well off. She herself was comfortable on a schoolteacher's salary, with a decent advance on royalties for her book. But this place represented wealth right out of her league. Wil was only a year older than she was—man, had their paths diverged. Maybe she should have dressed for this occasion, instead of wearing shorts and sandals. She told herself not to be so silly— he was still Wil—and buzzed the security device set in the sandstone pillar. The gates swung open.

Wil strode down the driveway to meet her. 'You're here,' he said, his relief obvious as he opened her car door for her. He looked impossibly handsome in khaki shorts and a black T-shirt. He also looked exhausted, his stubble halfway to a beard, dark circles around his eyes.

'I got here as fast as I could. How's Nina?'

'Hallelujah, the car trick worked,' he said, pumping his fists above his head in victory. 'She's asleep at last.'

Georgia swung her legs out of the car. 'You mean I've come all the way down here for nothing?' As she looked up at him, she pretended a pout of annoyance.

He shook his head. 'Not a wasted journey at all. Trust me, I need you.' For a moment she thought he might hug her.

She wanted him to hug her. She hugged her friends of both sexes all the time. Kissed them on the cheek. But not Wil. Never Wil. The 'no touching' rule, which neither of them had ever formally agreed to but had been there from the beginning, appeared to be still firmly in place. 'When it comes to Nina, you're a miracle worker,' he said.

'I'm not sure about that,' she said, bemused. 'I only suggested what my sisters do when they get desperate.'

'I don't have sisters to learn from. The staggering depth of my ignorance when it comes to babies is becoming all too apparent.'

'No luck with the online videos?' she said with a sly sideways look. Maybe teasing wasn't appropriate but she couldn't resist.

'A fail, I'm afraid,' he said with a hands-down gesture. His wry grin brought that irresistible dimple to life in his left cheek. 'It seems only miracle worker Georgie has the goods.'

'I hope I'll live up to expectations,' she said, determined not to feel too flattered. Liking to be needed was one thing, to be at the beck and call of someone quite another. It was a trap she'd fallen into one time too often. Including, at times in the past, with Wil.

'Come on in,' he said. 'But you have to walk on your tiptoes and talk in whispers.'

She laughed. 'You're learning fast,' she said. 'Do not wake slumbering baby at any cost.'

'Laugh out loud now,' he said dramatically. 'Once you enter these doors, make a noise at your peril.'

He put a finger to his lips as he led her through double carved wooden doors and into a spacious, marble-tiled entrance hall. Walking with an exaggerated tiptoe, he indicated for her to follow. She smothered another laugh, not with complete success, which earned her raised dark eyebrows and a mock glare. His reprimand only made her want to laugh more. Old Wil, playful Wil, was still there.

He indicated for her to follow him. As she did so, walking on tiptoe, she couldn't help but notice that his back view was as hot as ever: broad shoulders tapering to a perfect butt, long legs strong and tanned with just the right amount of dark hair. She took a deep breath and chanted to herself the familiar mantra: *just friends*—then repeated it again to make sure her libido got the message.

As she dutifully followed him, she forgot even the fabulousness of Wil's butt as she took in the fabulousness of his house. An interior designer had obviously been given a no-expense-spared budget. Every room deserved a place on the cover of a high-end interiors magazine. In the expansive, high-ceilinged living area, luxurious furniture was placed around an outsize fireplace set around with river stones. The house would be toasty warm in winter, but now air conditioning cooled the January heat to a blissful temperature. The kitchen was over-the-top, chef-equipped, but warm and inviting at the same time. The adjoining informal family room was just as elegantly decorated and furnished as the more formal areas.

Yet among the designer perfection, Georgia noticed heart-warming evidence of a baby in residence—a fold-up stroller in the entrance hall; in the family room a high chair; a tray of feeding bottles on the marble kitchen counter-top. And toys. The family room had soft toys and educational toys and baby books wherever she looked. For all the size and elegance of the interiors this was a family home. Wil's home with Nina. And, man, had he shopped for his baby! There was enough stuff here for triplets. Georgia smothered a giggle, successfully this time.

She followed Wil through folding glass doors to emerge onto an expansive deck that looked out across greenery and gardens, through to bushland and then the sea gleaming blue in the distance. There were no immediate neighbours in sight. A multimillion-dollar view.

The deck was sheltered under wide eaves and positioned to take advantage of sea breezes. Like the interiors, it was styled to magazine perfection, with vintage-style cane furniture, brightly coloured cushions, and a profusion of broad-leaved potted plants. On a level down to the right was an infinity-edge pool that seemed to stretch to the horizon, inviting her to plunge into its cool, aquamarine depths. Ahead of them sloped gardens with banks of hydrangeas blooming in multiple shades of lavender and blue. She breathed in the air, scented with the richness of frangipani, the sharpness of eucalypt, a hint of salt. And the indefinable tang of wealth.

She turned to Wil. 'Can we talk now?' she whispered.

'If we keep it low,' he said.

'I really want to shout *wow* at the top of my voice,' she said. 'Wil, this isn't a house, it's an estate.'

'More than five acres,' he said with a wave that encompassed the surrounding land and an unmistakable note of pride in his voice.

'Five acres so close to both the city and the beach.' She couldn't even imagine the multiples of millions it must be worth. That was when she noticed the tennis court. 'Not just an estate. Tennis court. Swimming pool. It's a resort.'

'But totally private, exclusively for the use of my family and friends,' he said. 'For you, the best is yet to come. Beyond the hedge are the stable complex and the arena.'

'And your horses?'

'In residence and waiting to be introduced to you.'

Excitement bubbled through her. 'I can't wait,' she whispered.

'We probably don't have to whisper out here,' he whispered back with a hint of dimple. 'Nina is sleeping in her room.'

He indicated the chairs set around a round table. 'Take a seat while I get us some drinks.' From an outdoor fridge disguised as a bench, he pulled out beers and mineral waters and placed them on the table along with some chilled glasses. 'I'm offering you a beer, but as you're driving I guess you'll want fizzy water as usual.' It appeared he still drank his beer straight from the long-neck bottle.

She accepted the cool drink, and Wil settled himself in the chair opposite her. He pulled out an intercom receiver from his pocket and placed it on the table in front of him.

'All the high-tech stuff to hand,' Georgia said. 'Just what I'd expect from an inventor.'

'There's a nanny cam in her room too,' he said.

'Of course there is.'

'Listen,' he said, putting his hand up. 'You can hear her breathing. I find it reassuring to know she's safe and secure under my watch.'

Georgia took in the rapt expression on his face, transcending the dark shadows and weary lines. 'You're a fully fledged dad already, aren't you?' she said softly.

'I was a dad the moment Nina looked at me

with those dark eyes, eyes I recognised from my mirror. The same eyes I think I remember my mama having. It was as if—' Abruptly, he stopped, as though realising he'd spoken about something he'd never shared with her before, and regretted it.

'It was as if what, Wil?'

His gaze didn't meet hers. Rather, he looked down at the monitor. 'Not important.'

'I think it is. As if you were with family again?'

Immediately, he went on the defence. As he had always done if she had dared to venture into any kind of discussion about his life before he was adopted. 'I have family. The best parents a man could have. The best brother. You don't have to be connected by blood to be family.'

'Yet your connection with Nina was immediate, intense.'

'And totally unexpected,' he said, finally looking up at her. 'It was as if we already knew each other. Took me completely by surprise.'

'I saw the resemblance immediately. She's like a mini Wil. You told me once you were only five when your birth parents died.' *Approach with caution.* She'd never pressed Wil on the details of his childhood. But now he was a father of a little girl who looked so like him her desire to know more overrode her usual restraint.

He clammed up. 'That's right.'

'Was it an accident?'

He paused, and she wondered if she would get an answer. 'They both drowned,' he said eventually.

'Oh, no, Wil.' Again she wanted to reach out to him, again she knew she couldn't.

'By all accounts, Mama wasn't a good swimmer. She got into trouble in the surf. My dad died trying to rescue her. Unsuccessfully, as it turned out.'

Georgia took a sharp intake of breath. 'What a tragedy.'

'I was there, on the beach. They found me wandering along the sand, crying out for my mama and daddy. Of course I don't remember much, just fragments. But it was all over the newspapers at the time. *"Little Boy Lost."* I read the accounts of the incident much later.'

Georgia clutched her hand to her heart. 'Oh, Wil. I… I have no words.' She was crying inside at the thought of young Wil, kindergarten age, wandering the beach in distress, looking for his parents. She envisaged him in a pair of wet swim shorts, legs streaked with sand and holding a little plastic bucket and spade, tears streaking down chubby childish cheeks and sobs putting hiccups in his voice as he called for his mummy.

'I try not to think about it,' he said gruffly. 'Being with Nina is making me relive stuff I would rather have left forgotten.'

Georgia was grateful that the connection with his baby daughter had been so profound it had opened up channels in Wil so he was, at last, willing to share his past with her. 'You were so young.' Her heart ached for that little boy, recognised his vulnerability in the adult Wil.

He nodded. His eyes had a distant look, as if he was talking about people he didn't know at all. Which, she supposed, he didn't. She thought back to when she had been five years old but couldn't dredge up many memories. Her parents and her sisters had always been there from her birth until right now and memories mingled with memories.

'Was there any other family? Grandparents?'

'My father's parents were dead. Mama's parents were from a traditional, strictly religious family and had disowned her. Much to their displeasure, my parents had never got married. They wanted nothing to do with me. There was only an aunt, my father's sister in

Melbourne. I went to live with her. It didn't work out.' His words were terse, his expression grim.

He so obviously didn't want to talk further about it but Georgia couldn't help herself. While the portal was open she felt compelled to probe. 'So then you got adopted by a lovely family.'

'After a while,' he said, not meeting her eyes.

'So in a way, it turned out okay in the end. As okay as it could considering the…the tragedy.'

'You could say that.'

Georgia waited for him to say more but was met by a heavy silence that stretched out for too long to be comfortable. She took a sip of her drink. 'Thank you for sharing that with me. I always got the impression you didn't want to talk about what had happened to you as a child.'

She'd never before got up the courage to pry behind the sky-high barrier he had put up against emotional intimacy. Not just to her. To all their friendship group. To his girlfriends— a number of whom had sobbed on her shoulder after the inevitable break-up, a process she had found excruciating as she'd imagined how she'd be feeling if it were her. That impossible-to-breach barrier had always made her glad she had kept any attraction to him so firmly in check. Until Angie, he'd evaded committed relationships. She'd begun to wonder if he was capable of them.

'I didn't. I don't. I don't often give my birth parents a thought. But Nina seemed immediately familiar. I looked at her and I recognised her. It was the weirdest thing. Brought back flickering thoughts of a smiling, loving face. Of laughter. Of a kind voice with an accent. My mama's family was eastern European—she was backpacking around Australia when she met my father and never went back home.'

'Did you ever try to find her family?'

Wil's face hardened. 'That would have seemed disloyal to my new family. Besides, if they were the kind of people who would abandon their daughter and their grandchild, I never want to meet them.'

'You're determined not to ever abandon your daughter.'

'Never. She lost her mum even earlier than I did mine. But she has me, and she won't grow up wondering where she came from.'

'Which is why you agreed to her keeping in touch with Sharyn. So she knows her mother's side of the family.'

He scowled. 'Don't mention that woman. She's already called me three times to check how Nina is settling in.'

'That's well meaning of her.'

'Or interfering, depending how you interpret it.'

'You're still committed to an ongoing relationship with her and her boys, for Nina's sake?'

'Of course, but not until I've established myself as her father. Bringing Nina up myself without interference is something I have to do. It would be easy enough for me to hire nannies around the clock and leave them to it. But I want her brought up by her parent—not an aunt, not a nanny.'

Georgia took another sip of her drink. Thought carefully about what she might say. Schoolteachers had a reputation for being bossy. She didn't want to be perceived that way. 'It's really worthy of you to think you can do it all by yourself, Wil. But I don't know that it's that easy.'

He sighed, a great heaving of broad, manly shoulders. 'I'm beginning to see that. I'm getting the hang of the changing, the feeding, getting her dressed, though I'm going to ask you to help me with her bath when she wakes up. But there's one thing I hadn't counted on,

Georgie.' He looked directly into her face and she was stunned by his perplexed expression, the sadness in his eyes.

'What's that, Wil?' she said carefully.

'I don't think my daughter likes me.'

CHAPTER FIVE

GEORGIA STARED AT WIL, stunned by his woebegone expression, shocked by his words. 'What on earth would make you say Nina doesn't like you?'

His mouth turned down in a half-scowl, not the full brooding Wil scowl but enough to indicate his disappointment and dismay. 'She might only be seven months old, but she's got quite the personality, my little Nina. She's made it very clear she's just putting up with me and she'd rather be somewhere else.' There was an edge of hurt to his voice he couldn't disguise—certainly not from Georgia.

'I'm sure that's not the case. Didn't you say you thought she recognised you, the way you recognised her? I don't know that I can make a judgement about the opinions of a baby her age. But I'm wondering...well, it might be...' She struggled to find a tactful way to say it. 'She's probably missing her mum and her aunty.'

The scowl deepened. 'I thought you might say that—and of course it crossed my mind. Maybe a dad really isn't enough. Not that I will ever give up trying to be the best dad I can possibly be. But she needs more than I can give her. Like the care of a woman in her life.'

'Perhaps. That's what she's used to. I'm no expert on babies, Wil, in spite of your faith in me. I believe a dad can fulfil her needs, but this particular little one is used to being parented by a woman. It might take her a while to adjust to the fact her sole carer is her father. And… I'm not sure how to put this but, in her own baby way, she must be grieving the loss of her mum.'

'Yeah, I get that. I just want to do what's best for her. If the best isn't me, then—'

Lights flashed on the monitor as it started to sound—grizzling baby whimpers that increased in crescendo. 'She's awake,' Georgia whispered.

'Here she goes again. She's only just got to sleep. What am I doing wrong, Georgie?' He seemed grey and drawn and she wondered how much sleep he'd got in the time since she'd last seen him.

'Nothing you're doing is "wrong",' she said. 'My older sisters say caring for a baby is a steeper learning curve than anything they did

at university or in their high-powered jobs.
Their husbands agree. They had their kids
with them from the day they were born—
you're starting well behind the starting gate.
Should we go to her?'

'Give her a moment to see if she settles
down,' he said. But as he finished speaking
Nina started to wail, an urgent cry for attention, increasing in crescendo, impossible to
ignore.

Georgia looked at Wil. 'Let's go,' he said at
the same time she did.

Georgia followed Wil across the living
room, down a corridor and through an open
door into Nina's room. The spacious room
had obviously started life as a guest room,
elegantly decorated and so luxurious a guest
would never want to leave. The cot, change
table and pretty pink alphabet floor rug made
it instantly a nursery.

Nina was sitting up in her high-sided white
cot. She wore a pink onesie printed with white
bunnies over her nappy. Her face was red and
tear-streaked, her dark hair damp and sticking up on end.

'Nina, sweetheart, it's okay, Daddy's here,'
said Wil.

Even through her concern for Nina, Georgia marvelled at the depth of affection in his

voice. Without a doubt, Wil had bonded with his daughter.

'She looks a picture of misery, poor little pet,' Georgia said.

'I know,' said Wil, wearily.

'Shall we try a different voice?' Georgia headed for the crib. 'That's a very big noise for such a little girl,' she cooed. Nina looked at her, blinked, stopped wailing, hiccupped, then settled into a lower volume grizzling.

Georgia turned to Wil. 'May I pick her up?'

'Please. Anything to keep the volume down.' He ran his hands through his hair so it stuck up on end. Which made him look as frazzled as his little daughter.

Georgia approached the cot. 'Remember me, Nina? I'm Georgia.'

Nina immediately quietened. When Georgia leaned down to pick her up, Nina went willingly into her arms. Nina wound her arms around Georgia's neck and looked into her face. Yes, her eyes were like Wil's eyes. She was definitely her father's daughter. But there was a difference. Nina was her own little person. They were Nina's eyes. And the expression in them made her believe Wil could be right about the strength of her personality.

'I think she likes you,' Wil said.

'I'm a different pair of arms, a distraction.'

'A female distraction.'

'There's that.' Georgia disengaged Nina's arms so she could look at her more closely. Gently, she smoothed back the damp wisps of dark hair from the baby's forehead. 'I wonder if she's teething?'

'I wondered that too,' he said. 'I typed in "why is my baby crying?" into a search engine and teething came up as a possible cause.'

Georgia ducked her head, kissed Nina's sweet little neck, so Wil wouldn't notice her smile. 'Did it?' she said. She enjoyed the way he took his new duties so seriously.

'But when I looked up "teething" she didn't seem to have those symptoms. A rash and frothing at the mouth. Hell, if she'd been frothing at the mouth I would have rushed her to hospital.'

'Me too,' she said, turning to look at him. 'Did it really say "frothing at the mouth", Wil? Surely not. That sounds more like rabies. Or poison.'

'Excessive drooling and foaming is what it said and that sounded alarming. Anyway, she didn't have a rash or swollen gums. So I don't think she's teething.'

'Your guess is as good as mine. Seriously. Just because I'm a woman doesn't mean I'm a baby expert. Just because you're a man, doesn't mean you can't be.'

Nina reached out and patted Georgia on the face with her tiny hand. Georgia immediately gave the baby her full attention and was rewarded with a gummy smile. 'Oh, you're such a sweet little thing,' she said. 'Your daughter is adorable, Wil.'

'Yes, she is,' said Wil with a catch to his voice that surprised her.

Georgia's head bent close to Nina's, his daughter's tiny hand on her cheek, her solemn dark eyes searching Georgia's face was a sight so entrancing Wil couldn't tear his gaze away. He wanted so desperately to believe he could be everything to the daughter he hadn't known he had. But perhaps that wasn't possible. He was prepared to spend any amount necessary to get her what she needed. Turn his life upside down so he could spend time with her. But he couldn't give her what she'd had with her mother and her aunt. What she was getting right now with Georgia. A woman's touch.

Georgia was a natural with Nina. His little girl was now all smiles and gurgles. Nina wouldn't be his daughter if she didn't respond to the illumination of Georgia's smile the way he always had—by basking in it. Watching his friend and his daughter together, he felt an unexpected shaft of emotion stab his heart. A sudden yearning for what might have been if, one past day, he had given into that long-simmering attraction to Georgia. If he'd found the courage to try, even knowing the risk she might have turned him down. Perhaps she might now be the mother of his child. An unexpected joy prodded him at that thought, impossible as it was.

He had damaged their friendship, and any hopes he'd had of one day it becoming something deeper, by his hasty and ill-advised marriage. He fought against the bitterness he felt towards Angie, not only for depriving him of the first months of Nina's life, but also for engineering his estrangement from Georgia by her jealousy. But whatever Angie's shortcomings, she had bequeathed him this wonderful little girl.

And Georgia, lovely Georgia, had accepted his explanation for why he had cut her from his life. To a point, she had forgiven him. But he knew the foundations for their new friendship were laid on shaky ground. She was reserved, holding back the wholeheartedness of her friendship that had always meant so much to him. Now Georgia didn't trust him. Whatever it took, he would win that trust back.

'Wil, are you a tongue-roller?' Georgia asked, still engaging totally with Nina.

'No,' he said, startled at the question.

'I am. I wonder about Nina.'

'It's an inherited tendency, isn't it?' he said. 'And not something I'd given a second's thought.'

Georgia poked her tongue out at Nina, then rolled it into a tube. Nina reacted with chortles of laughter. In return she poked out her tiny, pink, very flat tongue. It was Georgia's turn to laugh.

'No rolling. She either takes after you or is too young to be able to do it. I haven't a clue how old she'd need to be.' Nina poked her tongue out again, then dissolved into her delightful baby laughter again. 'Clever girl,' said Georgia, planting a kiss on his daughter's cheek.

Nina was delightful. So was Georgia. Relaxed, confident and utterly lovely. No wonder Nina was enchanted with her. No wonder she was loving being kissed by her. *He had never kissed Georgia.* Georgia glanced over to him. 'I think she's learned a new party trick,' she said. *Why had he never kissed Georgia?*

Her eyes met his in a moment of sheer mutual delight in his child. He smiled, not wanting to break the moment. She smiled back and he saw something he'd never seen before, something more than a shared complicity in the cuteness of his daughter. Something that made him want to keep on looking into her blue eyes until he could figure it out.

Then Nina seized upon Georgia's moment of inattention to tug at a lock of Georgia's hair. Georgia's laughter turned to squeals. 'Ouch! That's quite a grip you've got on you, young lady. Ouch!' Which only made Nina laugh more.

Wil laughed too. The tension that had been building since he had first found himself in this large, empty house with his baby daughter, and pretty much clueless except for an overwhelming desire to do everything right for her, started to ease.

Georgia. She was the answer. Georgia would know what to do. She had an instinct for children. It had led her to her career teaching them. To her hobby of drawing and now writing for them. And here she was with Nina, immediately bringing laughter into the rooms of the big empty house where he had lived alone.

Alone and, until now, glad of it. Angie hadn't been able to keep up her fun, loving act much past the honeymoon. He'd tried to understand how childhood abuse had shaped her and had made allowances for her behaviour. But life in the Pyrmont apartment had become hellish. She had insisted on knowing what he was doing every second of the day. There'd been tantrums and excesses of behaviour that had shocked him, then scared him. He'd longed for privacy, time for himself and a door he could lock behind him. He'd found it here. And vowed to stay single. How could he ever again trust his judgement when it came to a woman?

But he trusted Georgia. Believed in her innate goodness and honesty. Loved the energy she brought with her. *He had to keep her in his life.* And not just for Nina's sake.

Georgia gently disentangled her hair from his daughter's tiny fingers. 'I think she's inherited your strength,' she said with a wry smile.

'Good,' he said. 'I want her to be strong in every way.' During his years in the welfare system, he'd seen what could happen to vulnerable girls. He'd make sure his Nina would be able to hold her own whatever situation she found herself in. Like Georgia.

Georgia shifted Nina around so she rested comfortably on her hip in that instinctive way women did with babies. 'She's off to a good start, I reckon.'

'Nina is obviously at home with you,' he

said. 'You're right. She responds to a woman's touch.'

'It's what she's used to, Wil. She'll get used to you. But she might need more than two days to adjust.'

'I know you're right,' he said. 'I guess I don't like to admit she didn't fall for me as quickly as I fell for her.'

'I'm sure she will—just give her time. She's very relaxed and happy with you now.'

'Let's hope it stays that way, though I suspect it's because of you.' There was something so warm about Georgia that had drawn him to her from the get-go. His daughter seemed to feel it too.

'I'm a novelty. She seems a bright little thing. I suspect she might get bored easily. Why don't we take her outside? A change of person worked wonders. A change of scenery might too.'

'That's a thought,' he said. *We*. Georgia working alongside him to care for Nina seemed an eminently sensible option. Certainly for him and for Nina. But what would be in it for Georgia?

'Has she got a sunhat?' Georgia asked.

'It's hanging in the closet. I bought everything I thought she might need.'

Georgia walked over to the closet, Nina still

comfortable on her hip, and pulled open the door. Her laughter pealed out. 'Heavens, Wil, did you buy the baby store out? They mustn't have had any stock of cute outfits left after you visited.'

He shrugged. 'As I told you, the assistant was very helpful to a clueless father. Please note, while admiring my purchases, that each of Nina's garments is there in three sizes, one to fit now and two for when she grows bigger. That way I won't have to endure shopping for baby stuff for quite some time.

'Endure? Did you say *endure*?'

'You know I don't like shopping. What guy does?'

Did she, in fact, remember his loathing of shopping? During those two out-of-contact years, had she thought about him much at all?

Georgia had rarely been without an adoring boyfriend in tow, with another one waiting in the wings. It had seemed to him that as soon as the poor sucker had fallen for her, she'd finish with him. Which was another reason he'd been happy to keep her in the friend zone. Even in those rare times they'd both been single he'd never broached the possibility of more. He hadn't been ready for the commitment a relationship with her would demand. But apparently neither had she, in spite of what she'd often said about wanting the long-term and serious, the big white wedding. To his knowledge, she'd turned down two proposals. More now, perhaps.

He doubted she'd missed him. However, he had missed her and having her back in his life was more wonderful than even he could have imagined in those years he'd exiled himself from her warmth and positivity.

'But, Wil, shopping for a gorgeous baby like Nina would be a pleasure. I didn't like dolls when I was a kid, much preferred stuffed animal toys.' She dropped another kiss on his daughter's cheek. 'But a real-life baby girl is a different matter altogether. And, boy, have you got a choice of little outfits for her.'

He laughed. 'She's not a doll, Georgie.'

'But I'll have so much fun dressing her up,' she said. She pulled a tiny garment out of the closet. 'What about this adorable little shirt with the embroidered collar, Nina?' she said. 'It's hot out there and we need to protect you. You've inherited your daddy's olive skin but our Aussie sun in January can really burn.' Nina waved her arms about, reaching for the shirt, babbling as if she were trying to say something.

'Next time I shop for her, I'll invite you along,' Wil said.

'I'd love that. And Nina would come too, of course. I suspect she's going to have strong opinions of what she likes and dislikes.'

'Is that your professional, schoolteacher opinion?'

She paused with that thoughtful expression he knew so well of old. 'In a way, I guess so. Even on this brief acquaintance I can sense a strong personality.' She looked up at him. 'Like her dad. You've always been strong-minded.'

'I've had to be,' he said, not wanting to be further drawn. 'But right now this little girl just turns me to mush.'

'Me too,' she said. 'She really is a sweetie. Now, where's that hat?' She pulled out the pale pink baby-size fedora, popped it on Nina's head. 'This is the most adorable little hat I've ever seen. Did you choose it?'

'As a matter of fact I did,' he said, pleased at her reaction. 'I thought it was cool. Because I bought so much stuff at the baby store, the assistant threw it in for free.'

Nina took the fedora off her head and before Georgia could stop her had thrown it to the carpeted floor. His daughter's bottom lip jutted out in a way he was beginning to recognise. Georgia looked down at the hat, back to Nina and then up to Wil. Her expression was so dismayed he had to laugh.

How he'd missed her. He wanted to sweep her into his arms, Nina and all, and tell her that. But they'd always had a 'no touching' relationship, instigated, he realised, by him. There was a reason he'd never kissed her. Because he'd feared that hugging her, kissing her even in the most informal way, would unleash feelings he had thought he would not be able to handle.

'Well, I guess that tells us what your daughter thinks of our taste in hats,' Georgia said. She took out a tiny, wide-brimmed hat in white cotton.

'The shop assistant said that hat was more practical,' said Wil. 'What would I know?' The world of baby fashion was a mystery to him. He just wanted the best for his daughter and he could afford to give her the best.

'It ties under the chin so we might have more hope of keeping it on, mightn't we, little missy?' Nina went to grab it from her, but Georgia held it out of her reach. 'No hat, no walking down to see the horsies—uh, sorry, I mean horses.' She looked apologetically to Wil. 'That was a mistake for a schoolteacher to make. No baby talk if she's to develop proper language skills. Starting with the correct name for animals. We should make it a rule.'

'Of course,' he said. He hadn't really thought

about things like that. When it came to parenting, he had so much to learn. But with Georgia's input, it suddenly seemed a whole lot more achievable.

'Come on, Nina,' she said. 'Your dad and I are going to change you, dress you and introduce you to some special new friends.'

'Who do you think is going to be more excited at meeting these "friends"?' Wil said, making quote marks with his fingers. 'Nina or Georgia? I think I know who is dying to get down there and see the horses.'

'Of course I am,' she said, her mouth curving into a smile, her eyes dancing. 'You know me so well, don't you?' Their gazes held for a quick, glancing moment, an exchange of questions without answers.

Wil wasn't sure what to say in reply. Did he really know her any more?

'When it comes to horses, I think I know you well,' he said. 'Otherwise, I have some catching up to do. Starting from now.'

'You were right—again,' Wil said to Georgia not long afterwards. 'Nina is responding so well to a change of scene.'

'So am I,' said Georgia. 'I can't wait to meet Sultan and Calypso.'

As soon as he strapped Nina into the buggy—

who would have thought just days ago he would own a buggy?—and headed down the pathway to the stables she was alert and excited with no hint of a grizzle.

The two horses were grazing in the paddock under the shade of the eucalypt trees. At the sight of him, and with the possibility of treats, they came trotting over. He didn't disappoint them about the treats. He and Georgia fed them a carrot each, which they munched with gusto. Nina seemed to find the process fascinating, her little head turning from horse to horse, her arms flailing in excitement.

His horses seemed to know that Nina was an infant and stood placidly while he held his daughter close enough so she could pat their cheeks with her tiny hands. When she let out squeals of excitement, they didn't spook. The horses were on one side of the wooden fence, he, Nina and Georgia on the other. Horses could be flighty creatures and he didn't want to take any risks around his daughter and his friend.

He was getting used to the fiercely protective instincts his daughter aroused in him, which had sprung up the moment he'd looked into those dark eyes. As for Georgia, he had always been in the habit of watching out for her, whether they'd been around unpredictable horses or fending off unwanted admirers in a Sydney club. There had always been admirers. Right now, in denim shorts that showed off her long, toned legs and shapely behind and a T-shirt that made no secret of her curves, she was the tantalising blend of wholesome and sexy that men found appealing. He was no exception.

'So, what do you think of Sultan and Calypso?' he asked.

'They're beautiful. Well bred, well natured and well trained. And I think I sense a real rapport between them and Nina. You should encourage that. A love of animals is a good thing for a child. I think she loved them.'

'Is that a sneaky way of saying you'd like to see the horses again?'

'Perhaps.' Georgia gave him a mischievous sideways grin. 'But isn't this all about Nina?'

Was it? Suddenly it seemed to be as much about Georgia. About ways he could see more of her. Rebuild their friendship. Restore her trust in him. Georgia and Nina together seemed so right. He'd had too many years of refusing to let himself imagine how Georgia and Wil together as a couple might be, to allow that thought any real air time. Especially not now when his life had been turned upside down by the arrival of Nina.

Nina was back in her buggy and was happy for him to wheel her along as he showed Georgia the stable complex, which included four individual stables, a feed shed, tack room and a wash bay. Nina was very taken with the big ginger cat who lived in the stables. So was Georgia.

'I wonder if Nina has seen a cat before?' said Georgia. 'We don't really know what her experiences were in Katoomba.'

'She doesn't seem worried about the horses or the cat. The previous owners left him behind, so he came with the house,' he said. 'He's not the friendliest of felines, so we need to be careful.'

The cat had refused any overtures from Wil. The second Georgia called, 'Kitty, kitty,' the animal ran to her and wound around her legs in an ecstasy of purring. When Georgia picked him up to cuddle and then show Nina, the cat stood still and docile while his daughter patted him.

What was it about Georgia that had this aloof creature instantly besotted? Georgia was truly an exceptional person in every way. Had he been guilty of taking their friendship for granted all those years? Of thinking he could put anything deeper than friendship on ice until it suited him? That had all gone awry when she had met Toby and then he Angie. He'd made some very bad decisions.

'What a gorgeous big boy,' Georgia said, putting the cat down. 'He'll help keep the mice down in the feed shed.'

'He doesn't live on mice alone. My housekeeper feeds him every day.'

Georgia turned to him. 'You have a housekeeper? I wondered if you had help in a place this size.'

'She doesn't live in, rather comes in every weekday. I like my privacy. There's a gardener too. And a stable hand, a student who works here and lives in the apartment that's at the end of the stable complex.'

'This place is awesome. Nina is so lucky she can grow up here. You were so lucky, Wil, growing up on a farm where you could have your own horse.'

'I was very lucky,' he agreed.

If only she knew how different his life had been until he'd been adopted by the Hudson family. How damaged he'd been and how his new father had encouraged his interaction with horses as a form of therapy. But he still couldn't bring himself to reveal the truth about himself to Georgia. He'd shared some of it with Angie because she had told him she'd had a similar background, and she'd used it against him.

'It was my dream to have my own horse,' Georgia said wistfully.

'You can come and ride mine instead. They need more exercise than I can give them.'

'I might take you up on that,' she said. 'Be careful what you offer. You might wake up one day to find I'm living down in the stables, sharing a straw bed with the cat.'

'In that case, I would have words with the cat about him illegally subletting his stable.' She laughed. Nina started to chuckle too, not that she could have any idea of what was funny. It was just that Georgia's laughter was contagious. So he joined in the laughter too.

It was *so* good having her back. Even if he did have to battle the sudden image of Georgia in his bed that flashed into his mind. The cat could have his straw bed to itself. The thought of making love to Georgia was one he'd fought to keep at bay so many times over the years. If it were not for the complication of having Nina now in his life he might be thinking it was time to stop fighting those thoughts.

Georgia, thank heaven, was oblivious to his lascivious thoughts of her in his bed. She was instructing Nina on how to say goodbye to the kitty. He almost corrected her to say 'cat' not 'kitty' as per their new rule but decided against it.

'Next time Nina won't settle, bring her down here with all the distractions,' Georgia said. 'I guarantee she'll stop wailing.'

As he had to stop getting distracted by Georgia's legs in those abbreviated shorts. Or the swell of her breasts under the snug-fitting T-shirt.

He cleared his throat. 'Yeah. Good idea.'

He didn't want her to go.

As he pushed the buggy back up to the house, Georgia by his side, Wil's brain was whirring in hyper-drive, trying to think of ways he could entice Georgia to spend more time with him and Nina.

He was an inventor. An engineer. A creator of design solutions. He saw a problem, then found the solution. The problem in this case was obvious. Nina needed Georgia. He needed Georgia. By the time they reached the house he'd come up with an ideal solution.

CHAPTER SIX

WIL WAITED UNTIL a tuckered-out Nina had been fed, bathed and put to bed for her nap before he broached his idea to Georgia. They were sitting around the round marble-topped table in the family room, eating a late lunch of sushi and Japanese salad delivered from a favourite restaurant in the nearby beachside suburb of Narrabeen. The room looked out over the pool and was one of his favourite places in the house. To have Georgia sitting opposite him, relaxed and enjoying her lunch, made it even better. *She belonged here.*

'I seem to be grovelling with gratitude every time I speak to you,' he said. 'But I really want to thank you for your help with Nina today.'

She took a sip from her mineral water. 'Grovel away, I like it.' She smiled her lovely Georgia smile. 'Seriously, Nina is delightful and you're very welcome. It wasn't a hardship.'

'My daughter likes you,' he said.

'I hope so. I like her too,' she said.

Wil took a deep breath. 'It goes without saying that I like you.'

He was finding it difficult to believe that she was actually here in his home. Seeing her interact with his horses had brought back so many memories of the good times they'd shared over the years. He'd never met anyone else with whom he'd felt so at ease, supported and encouraged. When he'd bought the horses, he'd found himself wishing she'd been with him to give her opinion. Had he chosen Calypso with the thought in the back of his mind that one day Georgia might enjoy riding her? *How he'd missed her.*

She flushed high on her cheekbones; her eyelashes fluttered in the way that happened when she was disconcerted. 'I could say the same. About you, I mean. We go back a long way.'

'We do. And I'll grovel some more to say how glad I am that you didn't slam the door in my face when I turned up out of the blue on your doorstep two days ago.'

'I won't deny that I wanted to. But curiosity overrode caution. Then when you told me about Nina, I just had to listen to you.'

'I'm so glad you did. What a hit you proved to be with her. I suspected she would be comfortable with a woman caring for her. You proved that today.'

'That could be so.' Georgia paused. 'Perhaps you could reconsider your stance on a nanny, Wil?' Her expression was delightfully serious as she leaned across the table towards him. 'Why not get some help? There's no shame in it. No one but me would even know you're backtracking on your "parent only" stance. I had a nanny when I was young. I loved her.'

'You're right. I don't like to backtrack. I was determined to do everything myself. But I'm beginning to come to the same conclusion.'

Her eyes lit up. 'That's great, Wil. I'm so glad to hear that. Getting help won't detract from your role as her father. And I'm sure you'll be more relaxed and be able to enjoy getting to know your daughter.'

'Yes to all that,' he said.

'You'll have to get the right person, of course. Most importantly, make sure Nina is comfortable with her.'

'I know just the person for the job.'

Her eyes widened. 'Really? That's good. Who?'

'You,' he said.

Georgia put down her fork with a clatter on her plate. 'Me? Be your nanny?'

'It makes perfect sense. You're on holidays.

You said you needed extra cash for your vacation in July. I think I speak for Nina, too, that you would be the ideal person. Just until you go back to school. I should have everything sorted by then.'

Georgia stared at him without speaking for so long, he thought he'd shocked her speechless. The colour drained from her face, leaving her freckles stark against the creamy paleness of her skin, then flushed back warm and angry.

Wil had a sinking feeling that perhaps his idea for keeping Georgia close by might not have been one of his best ones.

Her eyes narrowed, sapphire ice in their coldness. 'You mean pay me?'

'That's the plan.'

'You become my employer?'

'I wouldn't put it like that.' This wasn't going quite as planned.

'You'd be paying me to work for you. That would make you my boss. What on earth made you think that was a good idea?'

He frowned. 'It makes sense. You got on so well with Nina. I really like having you here. From what you said you could do with the extra money. I'll offer a very generous salary. It will only be for three weeks. To help Nina get used to me. And vice versa. You could perhaps do weekends during term time if you wanted to if it worked out. I haven't really thought that far ahead. Right now, Nina needs you. I need you.'

She slowly shook her head as if in stunned bewilderment at his words. 'Wil, have you got more money than sense? We've only just reconnected as friends. I've spent two days helping you with Nina purely out of friendship. And you want to turn all that on its head by making my help into a financial transaction. Where I would have to answer to you, defer to you, hold back on speaking my mind. Working for friends is a terrible idea. I actually consider your offer of employment to be an insult.'

'It certainly wasn't meant that way,' he said slowly.

Georgia pushed her plate away from her and got up from the table. 'I think it's time I left you to it.' She glared at him. 'Look up nanny agencies and find your nanny that way.'

She was seething. He knew her well enough to know that. Unwittingly, he had hurt her feelings. If she walked out now he would never see her again. And he couldn't bear that. How had things gone so wrong, so quickly?

He pushed away from the table so quickly his chair fell backwards with a clatter onto the marble-tiled floor. He made no effort to retrieve it. 'No. Don't go.' He closed the distance between them with a few brisk strides, reached out and took her arm. His action brought her close, closer than he had been to her for a long, long time. So close he was aware of her scent, familiar and heady; the warmth of her skin.

She stilled under his touch. Shocked, he thought, at the fact he had actually touched her. Surprised, perhaps, at the strength of his grip on her arm. Immediately, he let her go. His grip left the impression of his fingers on her arm, pale on her lightly tanned skin. He took a step back from her so the distance between them was not as intimate or confronting. She glared back up at him but behind her combative stance, the icy accusation in her eyes, he could see her hurt.

'I didn't mean to insult you, Georgie. My offer was meant more as a compliment. Ever since you got here I've been trying to figure out how to get you to spend more time with me. I mean Nina. I mean me and Nina. Without taking advantage of your kindness and generous spirit, I mean.'

Dammit. Why didn't the words come out the way he wanted them to? He was usually so sure of himself when it came to negotiating a business deal. His shoulders sagged. That was the trouble. This wasn't about business. It was personal. And he'd gone about it in quite the wrong way.

'I don't work for friends, Wil. Golden rule. Of course, I'm dealing under the assumption that we are friends again. For the time being, anyway.'

'Of course we are,' he said. *More than friends.* There had always been a deeper bond than ordinary, everyday friendship with Georgia. For him, anyway. Perhaps because of the way it had started. Perhaps because it had never been entirely platonic with him. Perhaps there had always been an echo of *one day* about it for him.

That one day could very well be now. They were both single and unattached. Each facing a crossroads in their life. Now it looked as if he had messed it up—again. He had to make good on his mistake and keep her on his side.

Georgia fumed. She could scarcely look at Wil, she was so cranky. How could she ever have thought there was any chance of re-establishing friendship—or anything deeper—with New Wil when he had obviously moved so far away from Old Wil?

She and Wil had started as equals, both students. The scales could have tipped another way when he'd gone on that television show

and become a celebrity because of his clever-
ness and extraordinary good looks. He'd got
very wealthy, very quickly. His inventions had
kicked it off, then he'd made a killing in crypto
currencies. He'd upscaled his car and bought
the luxury apartment in Pyrmont. Started to
move in different circles. But still they'd stayed
pals. He'd never made her think she was lesser
because she was a schoolteacher on a salary
that would never make her rich.

Then Angie had come along and everything
had disintegrated. Actually, Toby had come before Angie and for a while there it had looked
as if she would marry before Wil. Two years
apart while Wil, it seemed, got even richer.
And acquired some more arrogance along the
way. *While she'd missed him every day.* She'd
thought that for all his wealth he was still the
same person who had been her best friend.
But now he obviously saw her in a different,
lesser light. As his inferior.

He looked bemused, his dark brows drawn
together. Did he not realise what was so wrong
with his offer? She'd sometimes wondered
about his emotional intelligence. Now she
was convinced he didn't read cues the same
as other people. What made him a brilliant engineer might not make him great in everyday
people transactions. Or so his ex-girlfriends

had told her as they had bewailed the way it had ended with him.

'I'm not for sale, Wil. What made you think I was?'

'I didn't think that for one moment,' he said. 'I saw it as a clever solution to a problem. A win-win situation. I couldn't entrust Nina to a stranger.'

Georgia felt slightly mollified by the sincerity of his expression. 'You know I can be trusted with Nina.' When his baby looked so like Wil, she was predisposed to be fond of her. Already she had fallen under Nina's spell.

Wil sighed. 'I hate to admit failure of any kind. But you can see that I'm barely treading water with her. I need help. You really are the only one I could trust with this little person who has become so important to me, so quickly.'

No way in the world would Georgia agree to be Nina's nanny. Yet she felt torn when she thought about the story of his birth parents Wil had finally shared with her. She shuddered at the thought of the accident that had deprived him of his family, sent a lost and lonely little guy into the harsh embrace of state care.

Yet he seemed to have grown up undamaged. She was touched by the way he had so immediately recognised that family in his little girl. How he had stood up to his responsibility, not grudgingly but with love. A lesser man might have walked away from a child bequeathed to him under such circumstances. There was much to admire in New Wil.

But that still didn't make her want to work for him. Under any circumstances.

'Surely there must be someone else you could trust with Nina?' she said. 'What about your parents?'

'Mum is thrilled at the news she's a grandparent. Dad too. But they're not here. They're at a wellness spa in Phuket.'

'Thailand. Nice.'

Wil's parents were wealthy farmers who ran the large, historic farm holding Five and a Half Mile Creek, near the border of New South Wales and Victoria. Over the years, Wil had said he would like to take her there but it had never happened.

'Yes and no. Mum hasn't been well.'

'Oh. I'm sorry to hear that.' Georgia had met his parents a few times over the years when they had visited their son in Sydney. She could see the struggle on Wil's face whether or not he should share the details with her. 'Is she okay now?'

'She's getting over chemotherapy. Breast cancer. She had a mastectomy last year.'

'I'm so sorry, Wil. Your mum is lovely. I liked her a lot when I met her.'

'The prognosis is good, thank heaven. She's in remission. But she needed a complete break. Relaxing. Eating well. Meditation. Mum being Mum, as soon as she started to feel better, she wanted to throw himself back into work. Dad had to take her away.'

'What about the farm?'

'My brother, Ned, is looking after things. He's in partnership with Dad now. He'll be taking over when Dad decides to hang up his boots and retire.'

'Okay, so obviously your mum can't help you with Nina. I'm glad to hear she's getting the rest she needs.'

'Which brings us back to you.'

She put up her hand to stop him. 'No, Wil. That doesn't bring us back to me.'

'Hear me out. Please.'

She glanced at her watch. Didn't really register what it said. 'I should be going.'

'Just five more minutes,' he said.

'Okay,' she said. 'And not a minute more.' She walked over to the family-room sofa where she had left her handbag. Sat down. Wil followed her to sit on the other sofa, placed opposite hers, a coffee table between them.

He leaned forward, elbows resting on his

knees, gaze not leaving her face. 'You're living at your parents' home, right? How long do you think it will last before you get in an argument with your dad?'

He knew her so well. Still. 'Maybe I've already had a difference of opinion,' she grudgingly acknowledged. 'I love Dad dearly but the second I'm back under the same roof we clash.'

'There must have been a reason you didn't move on to another shared household with your flatmates?'

'You mean apart from flatmate number one's ghastly boyfriends and flatmate number two's apparent allergy to housework?'

Wil indicated their luxurious surroundings with a sweep of his hand. 'So living here could possibly have some appeal. Your own bedroom and private bathroom, use of a swimming pool and tennis court. With the added attraction of horses and somewhere to ride them. Oh, and proximity to the beach as an added bonus. Plus a housekeeper, and commercial cleaners to do the heavy stuff. Isn't that an attractive proposition?'

'Very attractive.' This was, in every way, her dream house. Though he hadn't added, as an enticement, attractive man for company. 'That is, if I was in any way interested in working through the vacation. I mean, working on anything apart from the illustrations I have to have finished by the end of the month. My parents think of it as my "little hobby". But it's not a hobby. I'm being paid. I have a deadline to meet. It's a job.' She knew she was doing a rotten job of keeping the rising frustration out of her voice.

'You're fighting to be taken seriously. I get it.'

Of course he did. He always had got her frustration at being a creative person in a family of business-minded achievers. They'd talked her out of art school. She'd seen the common sense in getting her teaching degree and the subsequent steady income. But she'd never stopped sketching, painting and dreaming of making her art her life.

'I know you do,' she said. 'Now is my chance to do what I've always wanted to do. Maybe make it a full-time career.'

'I've still got every card you ever made for me,' he said. 'The birthday cards. The good luck cards. The congratulations cards. All Georgia Lang originals. All brilliant.'

'Really? You saved them?'

'They'll be worth something one day, I'm sure.'

If there ever was a moment she wanted to kiss Wil, this was it. And not a friendly peck on the cheek, either. Memories of all the good times they'd shared together came flooding back. Of how miserable she'd been without his presence in her life.

Wil leaned back into his sofa. She was struck again at how tired he looked. Although the dark shadows under his eyes, the shadow on his chin and the tousled hair only added to his appeal. He was hot. The hottest of the hot.

'I understand how important your art is to you,' he said, the tiredness apparent even in his voice. 'Of course you wouldn't want to be distracted by Nina. It was a mistake to ask you. I can muddle along on my own. Maybe Mum can stay with me when she gets back from her trip. And I hope you'll still visit me and Nina here when you can lift your head from your sketchbook.' He got up. 'I should let you go.'

She got up too, so hastily she nearly tripped over the coffee table. 'Wil. Wait.'

The bleak expression in his eyes made her heart contract. He thought he'd lost her. That she'd walk out of here and that would be it.

'I have an idea. Why don't you rewind to when we were eating our lunch and talking about what fun we'd had showing Nina the horses,' she said.

He narrowed his eyes. 'Rewind?'

'Start all over again. You don't ask me to work for you as your nanny. You take a different tack.'

He frowned. 'I'm not sure what you're getting at.'

'Listen and learn.' She started to pace up and down the room as she warmed to her subject, much as she sometimes did in her classroom. 'You say to me that, while Nina is adjusting to you as her primary carer, it might be nice to have some female help with her. Not a nanny, because you wouldn't trust a stranger with your precious daughter. You mention how Nina seems to like me. I say I like her.'

He nodded thoughtfully. 'Subtly different to what I actually did say.'

'Correct. This is a rewind, remember. You certainly don't insult me by making me an offer of employment.' Wil went to protest but she put her hand up to stop him. 'Instead you point out that I, Georgia, am on school vacation, have illustrations to finish, and am sure to go stir crazy living with my parents. You suggest that I move into this enormous house for the rest of the holidays as a housemate, on the understanding that I spend time with Nina. Out of friendship, it's understood, not for money. For the duration, I pay rent and—'

It was Wil's turn to put up his hand to stop

her. 'No rent. Now you insult me by suggesting such a commercial transaction. You're quite right, no money should exchange hands and sully the purity of our friendship.'

Taken aback, she stopped her pacing and looked at him. 'I couldn't have said it better. You've caught on completely.'

'I'm a fast learner.' He smiled a little smugly, which made her smile too. 'So then I say, you help me care for Nina in lieu of rent.'

'Quite right, too,' she said. 'I've never been a freeloader.'

'You've spelled out what I should say, Georgie. So what do you say in response?'

She looked up at him, at his handsome face, his dark eyes searching her face. This was Wil, her friend. Asking for her help in such a way she couldn't say no. She smiled but it was a bit wobbly at the edges. 'I say, "Why, Wil, what a fabulous idea. I would love to be your housemate and share this amazing house with you and Nina. Thank you for your kind offer."'

He drew those dark brows together; the dimple revealed itself in his left cheek. 'So that's a "yes"?'

'It most certainly is. When can I move in?'

A huge grin of relief spread across his face. 'Tomorrow.'

'It's a deal,' she said, her own grin less exuberant but as heartfelt. 'Shall we shake on it?'

She put out her hand in a businesslike manner for him to take. Then thought better of it. 'Heck, Wil. I don't want to shake hands. I want to hug you. But we never hug, do we?'

'No, we don't,' he said slowly.

'Why is that? When did we decide not to hug or even kiss each other on the cheek in greeting? Was it you? Was it me?'

'I suspect it was me, Georgie.' He looked down at her, his eyes half-lidded and sensual. The look she'd seen him give other women, but never her. He was looking at her not as his horse-riding buddy but as a woman. And letting her know he liked what he saw. Perhaps had always liked what he saw.

She felt breathless at the look in his eyes, had trouble choking out the words. 'Why was that, Wil?'

His voice was low and husky, intensely masculine. 'Because I couldn't trust myself not to want to kiss you for real. To kiss you and want so much more than kisses. I didn't trust myself to be able to hold back from something that might put off course the friendship I valued so much. I wasn't ready back then for where that might take us. Not with you, you were a keeper. And I wasn't ready for you. Not then.'

Her heart started to hammer so hard, she swore he must hear it. 'And I complied for the same reason,' she choked out. 'It was safer than starting something at the wrong time that might ignite, then burn out of control to leave us with nothing but the ashes of what we'd had. You always brutally dumped your girl-friends as soon as it got serious. Then I had them sobbing all over me. They thought I, as your friend, would know the secret of hanging on to you. But I didn't. By sticking to friend-ship, I got to keep you in my life.'

'You did the same to your boyfriends. As soon as the poor infatuated guy started to talk about happy-ever-afters, you ran. And you never stayed friends with them afterwards. They were consigned to oblivion. I didn't want to be tossed into oblivion if I kissed you and you liked it but then decided you didn't like it—or me—any more.'

'I didn't want to be dumped and have to say goodbye to our horse riding and the other things we shared that were so important to me.' Her voice threatened to seize up. 'I… I couldn't have borne to have lost you. We were better as friends than as…as lovers.'

'And now?' he said. His head lowered to hers as he took a step closer. So close she could feel the heat of his body, feel intoxicated by his scent both familiar and unfamiliar at the same time. Quite unconsciously, she swayed towards him, aching for his touch, frightened of it at the same time.

Panic grabbed her and she stepped back. 'Then you dumped me anyway. Even our friendship didn't protect me from that. And it hurt, Wil. It really, really hurt.'

'I'm sorry,' he said hoarsely. 'If I could make it up to you, I would.'

'I'm not sure we can go back to what we had. Or even if I want to. Or to risk moving on to something else. It's different now. We're different people. And there's Nina to complicate things. We're going to be sharing a house. And I'm still not sure I—'

Wil laughed. A low, husky laugh that ran shivers of awareness through her. *Wil as a lover.* She had never allowed herself to think about him in that way. *Now it was all she could think about.*

'So we keep the status quo?' he said. 'No touching, no kissing, no acknowledging at last that we both want more?'

'Um, yes.' She didn't want to think of him like that. It was too risky. He could hurt her too much.

'You're sure about that?' He picked up her hand as if to shake it. But his touch was not businesslike at all. He lazily circled the sensitive palm of her hand with long, strong fingers, unimaginably pleasurable. She shuddered. If holding her hand could make her feel like that, what would it be like to make love with him? *And then to lose him if it didn't work out.*

Her voice came out in a choked half-sob. 'I'm not sure about that at all,' she said. 'I… I'm scared, Wil.' Give in to impulse and she could end up with the horror of all heartbreaks.

'We could start with a hug,' he said. 'A friendly hug.'

She thought of all the hugs she'd avoided with him over the years. Things were different now. How could a hug do any harm?

He drew her close, wrapping his arms around her tenderly as if she were something precious and valuable. She hugged him back and, for a brief moment, laid her head against his shoulder. His breath was warm and ragged against her cheek. Pressed against the hard wall of his chest, she was aware of the rapid beating of his heart.

'Just a friendly hug,' she echoed. 'Why didn't we do that years ago instead of making such a big deal of it?'

He cleared his throat. 'A harmless hug,' he said as he dropped his arms and she stepped back from him.

'Didn't feel a thing,' she lied, hoping the overbright tone of her voice didn't give her away, knowing that Wil could still read her as well as he ever had, and hoping he wouldn't use that knowledge to hurt her.

But as she drew away from the hug, the vulnerability in his eyes was visible for a fraction of a second before he masked it with a smile and that disarming dimple. She became aware she also had the power to hurt him. And that was equally terrifying.

CHAPTER SEVEN

THE NEXT DAY Georgia was running late on her way to Wil's house, her first day as his house-mate. It was already mid-morning, later than she'd intended to move in and get unpacked. As it was Saturday, her parents were at home and had demanded to know why she was moving out of the family home when she'd only just moved back in.

When she'd told her mother about Wil and Nina, the attitude had changed. Dear Wil was a widower now? Technically he was a divorcee but they obviously thought widower sounded more romantic. Of course Georgia must move down to Ingleside and help him and his little girl. They'd always liked him so much. Thought it such a shame she and Wil had never dated. Wil had always been a 'catch'. Now that he was so wealthy in his own right, even more so. It was no use protesting that she and Wil were just friends and had never been anything more. Her mother had laughed, as if that were the most amusing thing Georgia had ever said. 'You two were perfect for each other—only neither of you could ever see it,' she'd said.

Maybe we did see it, Georgia thought afterwards as she drove down to the northern beaches. *Saw it and ran from it, too scared of changing the status quo. We missed our chance.*

Could there be a second chance for them?

She hadn't been able to stop thinking about how she'd felt in Wil's arms the day before. *'A harmless hug.'* It could never be 'just a hug' with Wil. Not now that the awareness that had simmered underneath their platonic friendship had been acknowledged. Nothing and everything had changed since they'd made the unspoken 'no touching' pact. Fact was, she was no more ready for a relationship with Wil now than she had been when she was nineteen. And he certainly wouldn't be promising commitment any more than he had then.

Maybe there'd been a chance with Old Wil if they'd got their timings right. However New Wil came as a package deal. No longer was it just about him. Now every decision Wil made would have to be made with Nina in mind. Particularly when it came to women. As it should be. He would have to be extremely careful who he let into his life. Nina's safety, Nina's welfare had to be paramount. Already, she herself felt that about his enchanting little daughter.

Then there were her secret deep-down fears when it came to her and Wil. *If* anything were likely to happen between them. Nina was an eminently lovable little person. But to be thrown into motherhood headfirst would be a scary thought. Georgia had never dated a man with a child. She wasn't sure how she felt about being a stepmother. Would she be able to love Nina as deeply as she would love a child she bore herself? What if other children came along?

Even in just a few days she was starting to care for Nina. To step further than friendship with Wil would now be doubly dangerous. Double the risk to her heart. If she'd been too wary to risk a relationship before for fear of losing him altogether, how much riskier would it be now? If things went wrong, she'd lose not just Wil but Nina too. And Nina would suffer from the loss of another mother figure from her life.

For her and Wil, there could only be a friends-with-benefits arrangement. And she certainly didn't want that—certain heartbreak lay at the end of that path. Double heartbreak where Nina was concerned.

Far better to have Wil and Nina as part of her life, but not the focus of her life.

Friends. That was what they did well. That was the way it should stay. *Without benefits.*

Driving in Sydney on Saturday meant negotiating streets blocked with the vehicles of hordes of parents transporting kids to school sport venues all across the city and suburbs. By the time Georgia drove through the gates to Wil's house—home for the next three weeks—she was feeling decidedly frazzled. A dip in that glorious pool as soon as she got there might be just what she needed.

Wil had given her the passcode for the gates and the security keys for the door. As she pushed open the front door her phone buzzed. She paused to check it. A few missed calls. All from Wil. No point in picking up now. She'd be seeing him in just a minute.

As Georgia headed into the hallway she prepared an explanation for why she was later than expected. An explanation that did not include outrageous levels of matchmaking from her mother. Then she paused when she heard voices. Wil hadn't said he was expecting visitors.

To have other people there wasn't a bad thing. In fact she was relieved. Conversation might cover any awkward moments between her and Wil on the occasion of her actually moving into his house. Especially after that hug the day before. And her sleepless night pondering and discarding possible scenarios that involved her and Wil in something rather more intimate than a hug.

But the last people she expected to see when she walked into the family room were Wil's parents, sitting around the table where she and Wil had had lunch the day before. A teapot and cups were set there and plates of cake and cookies. Nina was in her high chair, gnawing on a baby rusk.

'Georgie.' Immediately he noticed her, and Wil got up from his chair. Her heart did the familiar flip. In long shorts and a dark T-shirt, he was heart-stoppingly handsome. She remembered how good it had felt to be held close to his chest in that fleeting 'just a hug'. How would she be able to keep her hands off him? 'We've been waiting for you,' he said. 'Did you get my calls?' His expression told her she should have listened to his messages.

'Sorry, no,' she said, puzzled and unable to read the silent message he was trying to send her via the raising of his eyebrows and the nod in the direction of his mother. 'I had my phone muted to placate my father, who has a thing about mobile phone addiction, and forgot to unmute it.'

Wil's mum and dad sat on either side of the high chair, smiling adoringly at Nina, who was waving the half-chewed rusk around like a conductor. They looked up at Georgia, their smiles embracing her too. Georgia smiled back with genuine pleasure. She'd last seen them three years back when they'd treated Wil and a group of his friends to dinner at an exclusive harbour-side restaurant.

Now she had to hide her shock at the change in Wil's mother. She'd been slim before but now she was bone-thin. Her hair that had once been tinted blond was now a dull grey. Even her hazel eyes seemed faded. Where once she had been vibrant, now she seemed fragile. No wonder her family had wanted her to recuperate and be looked after at a luxury resort after the ordeals of chemotherapy and surgery. Wil's dad was tall and stocky with thinning ginger hair and the sun-reddened skin and faded blue eyes of a man with Scottish ancestry who'd spent his life farming outdoors in the harsh Australian climate. He'd aged too, more than the years warranted.

'Mrs Hudson, Mr Hudson,' Georgia said. 'So nice to see you.'

'Please. It's Jackie and Dave,' said Wil's mum as his parents got up from the table. 'Now that we're family.'

Family? How did becoming Wil's new housemate translate to *family*? A loose interpretation, Georgia supposed. Someone to care for Nina, help Wil adjust to fatherhood? But it was a big jump from friendship to family. 'Jackie and Dave,' she murmured obediently.

Jackie gave her a hug, warm and genuine. 'I was so thrilled at your news. To hear I have a granddaughter one day and then just days later to discover you and Wil are engaged to be married. I couldn't be happier. It's almost too much excitement to deal with.'

Engaged?

'Er,' Georgia choked out, frantically looking to Wil for an explanation.

She stepped politely back from Jackie's embrace, fisted her hands by her sides, forced a smile. Could Wil see the steam coming from her ears? Surely he hadn't pulled that stunt on her again? If so, she was going to turn around and drive straight back to Lindfield.

Wil came to stand beside her, brushed his hand against hers, caught her eye. He read her annoyance. She read the response in his eyes and the slight shrug of his shoulders: *not my fault*. 'Mum and Dad were in Phuket when I called to tell them about Nina. I thought they were still there.'

'There's only so much lying about the pool, drinking vegetable juices and nibbling on exotic fruits a person can take,' said Jackie. 'We certainly weren't hanging around once we discovered we had a grandbaby to meet. We got the first flight out we could so we could meet Nina, a.s.a.p. What a little treasure she is.'

'Jackie thought it would be nice to surprise Wil,' said Dave.

'You certainly did that, Dad,' Wil said, his eyes still connected to Georgia in silent conversation. 'I had no idea until you and Mum turned up on the doorstep.'

Jackie continued, 'Of course, once we got to Sydney, we had to call Angie's sister to offer our condolences. Such tragedy amidst our joy.'

'Of course,' Georgia murmured through gritted teeth, still looking to Wil with a silent plea. *Get me out of this.*

'Sharyn told us the good news about you two being engaged,' Jackie said. 'Why we had to hear it from her and not Wil, I don't know.' She looked pointedly at her son in reprimand.

'We, uh, wanted to tell you face to face,' said Wil.

'I suppose so,' Jackie said, not sounding in the slightest bit mollified. 'But with important news like that we would have liked to hear it straight from you and Georgia.'

'It's only been a recent development,' Wil said. 'Just days, in fact.'

Georgia refused to jump in and help him out.

'No matter, we're absolutely delighted,' said Jackie. 'We always liked you, Georgia. Had hopes… Well, had hopes this might have happened years ago. Instead—I don't wish to speak ill of the dead—there was Angie, who wasn't right for our Wil at all. I'm glad you two finally saw sense.'

'Uh, thank you,' said Georgia. The effort of pasting on a fake smile actually hurt.

'We're over the moon, actually. You deserve happiness, son. We think you're perfect for him, Georgia, and you'll be getting a marvellous husband in Wil.'

Husband! Georgia gritted her teeth. This was getting completely out of hand.

'Thank you, Jackie. That's very kind of you. But could you excuse me for a moment? I need Wil's help to bring my bags in from the car.' She'd left her stuff—just the three drawers' worth—in the car, until Wil showed her which room would be hers for the duration of her stay.

'Let me help, too, son,' said Dave taking a step towards Wil.

'No need, Dad,' said Wil. 'You keep Nina entertained. She's very taken with her grandma and granddad.'

Georgia didn't say a word to Wil until they were outside in the driveway, beside where her car was parked, the solid double doors closed behind them. Then she whipped around to glare at him.

'What the heck, Wil? Why didn't you tell them we're not really engaged? Why am I caught up in this fake-fiancée farce again?'

'I was as shocked as you were. Who knew they would ever contact Sharyn? I started to explain but Mum was bubbling along about how happy she was, and I couldn't get a word in edgeways. Then she said that the news about our engagement, on top of the joy about Nina, gave her something to live for. I just didn't have the heart to disillusion her. Mum has been so unwell, Georgie. We thought we might lose her last year.'

'That's really sad, and I can see how worried you must have been, but *this*. No good can come of deception on this scale. I say we march right back in there and tell them it's a complete misunderstanding before it goes any further.'

He groaned. 'Can you play along just for a few days? Phuket was a stop for them, on the way to Italy, where they're booked into a villa in Tuscany with her sister. They're only here until Wednesday. She's so happy at the thought of us together.'

Georgia closed her eyes in exasperation. When she opened them it was to see Wil with hands gripped together as if in prayer and one knee bent in mock supplication. She couldn't help but laugh. 'No, Wil. Beg all you like. I won't be a part of this. It's madness. Blame it on Sharyn if you want. Say she got it wrong.'

He didn't laugh. Rather, he straightened up with a sigh. 'I'll tell them the truth when we go back inside.'

'Good,' she said. 'I'll get my bags from the car.'

'Wait.' Wil put his hand on her arm to stop her. The third time he'd touched her. The third time she'd realised how much she liked his touch. How she had to block her desire for more of his touch.

He cleared his throat. 'Before we go back in, there's something I need to fill you in on. It's actually another reason my parents are so delighted about our "engagement". Apart from the fact they've always liked you, that is.'

Georgia frowned at the seriousness of his tone. 'Fire away,' she said with a sense of foreboding, that something was about to change. As she waited she was aware of the splash of the fountain, the raucous squawk of rainbow lorikeets feasting on the orange flowers of a grevillea bush, the incessant background thrum of cicadas. The sun was warm on her shoulders in her sleeveless sundress and she pushed her hair, damp with humidity, away from her neck.

Finally, Wil spoke. 'It's something I've never told you before but they will expect you would know. The reason Mum is so over the top about all this.' He looked down at the ground, where he kicked the gravel with the toe of his canvas shoe. 'She so wants me to have a normal life and…and to be loved.'

'What do you mean? You have a great life. A millionaire's privileged life. One that many would envy.' She couldn't speak with any authority about how well he'd been loved.

'It wasn't always that way.' He looked back to face her. 'I've let you think I was adopted when I was five years old after my birth parents died, after I ran away from my aunt so many times she relinquished custody of me.

I've let all the friends I made after I moved to Sydney believe that.'

She frowned. 'But it wasn't true?'

'An angry five-year-old runaway boy isn't high on an adoptive parent's wish list. I was in and out of foster homes and children's homes for years. Some okay. Some very much not okay.'

She couldn't help her shocked gasp. 'Wil. How awful. Why didn't you ever tell me?'

'I wanted to put it behind me,' he said tersely.

'So when did Jackie and David adopt you?'

'The year I turned fourteen. When I was thirteen, I was incarcerated in a children's home in Melbourne. I say incarcerated because it was like a prison to me. That year, Jackie and Dave decided to take a child from the institution for Christmas to give a deprived city kid like me a holiday in the country.'

'Do people do that?'

'Kind people like them do. They were taking a risk with me. I had a reputation for being a troublemaker. The manager tried to talk them out of choosing me. But they told me later they saw something in me that no one else seemed to see and they insisted. Me or no one.' He looked hot and uncomfortable, and she realised how difficult this was for him.

'How wonderful,' she said slowly. Why had Wil never shared this?

'I thought it was wonderful, all right. I had every intention of running away as soon as I could, hitching a ride on a truck and never going back to that place I hated.'

'But you didn't.'

'I loved it there. Five and a Half Mile Creek was like heaven. Jackie and Dave knew just how to handle me. Dave told me later it wasn't much different from taming an unbroken horse using the kind, natural horsemanship methods he preferred. And I got on really well with Ned, their only child, who is six months older than me.'

Georgia had never met Ned, but Wil had always spoken of him with affection and regard. 'That was fortunate,' she said. 'It could easily have gone the other way.'

'He didn't resent me, the intruder with an attitude. Ned has the same quiet strength and confidence as his father. He told me he got lonely over the long summer vacation and welcomed the company of another teenager. At the end of the holidays, he begged them not to send me back. My parents are the type of people who should have had a brood of kids but they couldn't. Cut a long story short, by the time I turned fourteen they'd adopted me and I became part of their family. During term time, I was sent to boarding school in Melbourne with Ned. That was a challenge. But Ned looked out for me. I was a year behind him as I needed to catch up on my broken schooling.' He paused. 'I really hit the jackpot when they took me home with them.'

Georgia was so taken aback by Wil's story she was finding it hard to keep steady. It explained so many things. The feeling she'd always had that he was holding back. His difficulty in sustaining relationships. That emotional distance. Her heart ached for the troubled boy he must have been. 'Why tell me this now?'

'My parents will assume you know. I didn't want any awkwardness.'

'You mean apart from any awkwardness around pretending to be engaged?'

'Yeah. That. Mum will be disappointed but she'll get over it. She thought my past had made it difficult for me to…to, well, love. When she thought she might die, she feared leaving me behind to make another bad choice like Angie. Or be on my own. That's why she was so overjoyed about us. But you're quite right, it's best she finds out now it was a misunderstanding. She might be more disappointed if we leave it until further down the track.' He took a step towards the car. 'Come on. Let's get your bags. They'll be wondering where we are.'

Georgia stayed where she was. 'You sure know how to tug on the emotional heart-strings. After hearing that, how on earth can I possibly disillusion your lovely mum if the thought of you being happily engaged is sustaining her in a struggle with cancer?'

He shrugged. 'I don't mean to do that, Georgie. Just stating facts. I don't regret using the engagement tactic with Sharyn.' She'd puzzled over that at the time; now she knew where he got his fear of the welfare system. 'However, I do regret my parents finding out the way they did. I never dreamed they'd contact her.'

'Guess that's the type of kind, well-mannered people they are.'

'You're right about that,' he said.

'How long did you say they're staying?'

'Just until Wednesday. Then they take off for Italy to resume their holiday.'

She sighed. 'I suppose we could fake it until then. While they're in Italy, you can tell them it didn't work out.'

'Which wouldn't surprise them at all, with my history,' he said with a downward twist to his mouth.

Georgia ached to find out just what had gone

wrong with Angie, but now wasn't the time to ask. 'They'll still have Nina, remember.'

'Yeah. And maybe we should leave it at that. You're right about the deception. I don't like lying.'

'I'll lie too if you think it's that important to your mum.'

'Really?' He looked down into her face and she could see more than weariness in his eyes. He had had it so much tougher than she had ever imagined. He'd masked it so well during the years they had been friends. And she had the feeling that she still didn't know the whole story. 'You'd do that for me?' he said.

She nodded, finding it difficult to keep up a cool façade when inside she was crying at what Wil had gone through, at what he hadn't said about his time in the welfare system. During her training she'd taught in some disadvantaged areas around the state. She'd heard the horror stories. She'd seen some of the sad outcomes in her classrooms. Heaven knew what fate Jackie and Dave had saved Wil from. 'I couldn't bear it if some action of mine compromised your mother's recovery.'

'I'll really owe you after this, Georgie.'

'Yeah. You will. I'll need time to think about how you can repay me.' Her attempt at light-hearted humour fell flat.

'Thank you,' he said simply. He briefly put his hand on her shoulder. *Touch number four.* Then took a step towards the car. 'Okay. So let me get your things from the car so I can take them to our room.'

Georgia stared at him. 'Stop right there. What do you mean *our* room?'

CHAPTER EIGHT

WIL THOUGHT HE had stunned Georgia into a total state of shock she stared at him for so long, her blue eyes wide with disbelief. He wished he'd had time to talk this through properly with her.

She put up her hand. He noticed it was trembling. From anger? Fear? He doubted it was from excitement at the prospect of sharing a bedroom with him. Not now.

'Correct me if I'm wrong,' she said, 'but wasn't it our agreement that I have my own bedroom and bathroom? With just me sleeping in it?'

'That was our agreement,' he said. 'Our housemate agreement. Of course, things would be different for an engaged couple agreement. My parents would think it odd if my fiancée didn't sleep in my room with me.'

'Your fake fiancée, you mean,' she hissed. 'Whom you have never even kissed, let alone…

let alone done things engaged people might do in…in bed.' She cursed under her breath, which shocked him more than anything else she might have done. Georgia rarely swore.

'You wouldn't have to share my bed.' The sudden vision of a naked Georgia in his bed smiling, teasing, inviting him to join her on his cool sheets, made him catch his breath. And force his body not to react. 'If you don't want to, that is.'

Her eyes flared. He wondered if she might have had the same thought of how it might be in his bed with him. There was a sensual heat flaming within her righteous anger. He couldn't help but observe that the cotton sundress she wore, all splashes of orange and yellow, wrapped around her waist. It would be easy to untie it and have it slide down her body. What underwear did Georgia wear? Plain and practical, he surmised. Not that it would stay on for long if— *Stop!*

'Of course I don't want to,' she said. 'You can sleep on the floor.'

'That won't be necessary,' he said. 'There's a sofa I can bunk down on. Alternatively, once the lights were out, I could head on down to the stables and take your place with the cat.'

'What?' Her reaction was half stifled laugh, half disbelief.

'I know. The cat will be disappointed I'm not you. It hates me. He'll stalk off and I'll have the straw to myself. Bit scratchy, probably.'

'This is serious, Wil.' She reprimanded him with her best schoolteacher manner. He wondered if any of the lads in her class had crushes on her. He certainly would have.

'Sorry,' he said, not in the slightest bit sorry at raising a laugh from her.

'You're assuming I will agree to this revised arrangement. I'd rather have a room on my own. After all, we're only meant to be engaged. Not married. Your parents might actually approve that we're in separate rooms.'

'Unlikely,' he said. 'They're very broadminded. But the room-of-your-own thing isn't going to happen anyway. Not while my parents are here. There are six bedrooms but they're not all set up as actual bedrooms with beds in them. There's mine, of course; the room that's now Nina's nursery; and the one I'd earmarked for you. Mum and Dad have taken that one as they always use it. In fact, Mum decorated it for her taste.'

'What do you mean by that?'

'She's an interior designer. Mum is responsible for all the interiors in this house. Many years ago she was employed to go up from

Melbourne to redecorate at Five and a Half Mile Creek after Dad inherited. She fell in love with the client and never left.'

'Jackie is very talented. I love everything she's done. And that's a very romantic story. But I still don't want to share a room with you. No matter how beautifully decorated. Why don't we get some bedroom furniture delivered from a furniture store in time for tonight? Problem solved.'

'Do you seriously think that's going to happen between now and bedtime?'

'Throw money at the shop and it might.'

Did she hate the idea of sharing a room with him so much? 'We've shared a room before, Georgie.'

She scuffed the gravel with the toe of her espadrille. The shoe laced around her ankles with wide, white ribbons. She was all wrapped up like a beautiful gift. 'It was different then…' She cleared her throat and looked up at him. Her cheeks were flushed. Just as they'd flushed in his fantasy of her naked in his bed.

'I know,' was all the response he could come up with. Sharing a room with Georgia without wanting her in his bed for real would be a challenge. The stable was looking more and more like a viable option.

'The last room I remember sharing with you was the back of a horse trailer parked at a rural showground,' she said. 'We were both wearing riding breeches and boots and had our sleeping bags laid out on the top of the horses' straw.'

'I still remember. We had leased those good horses we competed on. How could I ever forget the aroma of our sleeping quarters?'

She wrinkled up her nose. 'The smell of horse lingered. No matter how carefully we'd swept the floor.'

'But we wanted our horses nearby and we figured the trailer would be more comfortable than a tent.'

He'd never forgotten waking before Georgia had. She'd been lying on her back with her arms flung behind her head, the sleeping bag tucked right up to her chin. It had been so cold in the trailer she'd been wearing her riding gloves and he'd been able to see her breath in tiny puffs of white vapour. During the night, her wavy hair had come loose and a shaft of early morning sun had illuminated her face and picked up auburn glints that had shone in the gloom of the trailer. Her expression had been peaceful, her lips slightly parted. She had trusted him and felt totally safe. *That was how she had to feel with him now.*

Back then, he'd had to fight the urge to

trace her features with his fingers, learning the shape of her pretty ears, her nose she despaired of because it wasn't quite straight, her mouth with the slightly irregular cupid's bow. Then to kiss her, the way he'd fantasised about so many times. There'd been a long piece of straw caught up in the wisps of hair around her temple. Gently, being careful not to wake her, he'd reached over to lift it out.

But he hadn't been careful enough. Her eyes had opened and slowly focused on him. For a long moment her gaze had connected with his. Then she'd smiled, a slow, lazy, sweet smile. 'Thank you,' she'd murmured. Then she'd closed her eyes again and within seconds had resumed her rhythmic breathing. Whether or not she actually went back to sleep, Wil had never known. Or that she'd even remembered waking to see him so close. Nor did he ever know whether the 'thank you' had been for him taking the straw from her hair, or for not kissing her and complicating their easy friendship.

He'd kept that piece of straw in the pocket of his riding jacket for a long time afterwards, only losing it because he'd once forgotten to remove it before he'd sent the jacket to the dry cleaner.

There'd been a few of those type of 'maybe'

moments throughout the years of their friendship. The mutual, unspoken acknowledgment that there could be something more between them. The 'one day' promise he had perhaps been guilty of hanging on to. Until the day, with eyes sparkling, she'd told him she thought she'd met 'The One' she might marry. Friendly, fun Toby, who had doted on her and let it be known in a not unsubtle male way that any other guy had better back right off. Even a so-called platonic 'friend'. Not long after that, Wil had met Angie.

'You'd better hope your sofa is more comfortable than the floor of that horse trailer,' Georgia said now.

She turned and started to stomp back towards the house. Wil caught her arm and pulled her back to face him. He grinned. 'I suggest you ditch that scowl if you're going to make our engagement seem believable.'

'Hmmph,' she muttered.

'In fact you might want to look friendly, affectionate and even, dare I say it, loving.'

'*Loving*, Wil? That particular emotion might be rather difficult to conjure up, considering the situation you've shoved me into.'

'Maybe a touch of passion might be in order.'

'Passion?' That would not be difficult for

him to feign. The sudden flare in her eyes told him it might not be impossible for her either.

'The only passion I'm feeling towards you at the moment, Wil Hudson, is of the angry kind. Anger for putting me in this position. When I was trying to do you and your mum a good deed. Sharing a room was not part of the deal.'

'But pretending we're crazy about each other enough to want to get married is.'

Her eyes narrowed. 'Time for a new rule that has nothing to do with the language we use with Nina. I'm talking about PDA only while in the direct presence of your parents.'

'You mean Public Displays of Affection?' he said.

'Correct.' He liked the way she said *correct* like the schoolteacher she was. She'd always been a little bossy, and he'd always liked it. 'And there's to be none of the other type of PDA.'

'Other type?'

'Private Displays of Affection. I mean, there can't be any. We really do have to return to the status quo when we're alone.'

'The old "no touching" way? Forget the friendly hugs?'

'Yes.' Her voice broke. 'I won't be able to deal with it otherwise. Last night we both admitted we had used the old way as protection.

I… I still need that protection. The hug… Well, it seemed more than friendly to me. We have to be platonic in private when we're pretending to be engaged. If those first kind of PDAs spill over and become the second kind, we won't know where we stand and it could get very awkward and…and hurtful.'

'You're scared,' he said slowly.

'I told you that last night,' she said a little stiffly. 'I really value you as a friend. We've only just found each other again and I don't want to mess it up. This fake-fiancée thing complicates everything.'

'Yeah. It does.' Adjusting to his new life with Nina was change enough on a momentous scale. After his disastrous marriage, he certainly couldn't see himself rushing into another permanent relationship, especially considering what that might mean to Nina. And a no-strings fling with Georgia where he kissed her goodbye when it ended was unthinkable. The friend zone was still the best place for them. The safe zone.

'I'm glad we're thinking the same way,' she said.

He looked back to Georgia. 'While this is theoretically a private moment. Perhaps we should think about the public moments. About how we handle it when—'

She screwed up her face and, for an alarming moment, he thought she might cry. 'This is crazy, Wil. Pretend engagement. Fake fiancée. Mapping out fake shows of affection. We're not those people out of some…some rom-com. We're straight-talking horse people.' Her voice broke on a half sob and she buried her face in her hands. 'I want to walk inside and tell your parents that Sharyn mistook fiancée for friend. Then I think how frail your mum looks, how the thought of you finding love gives her something to live for and—'

'Georgie, look at me.'

She dropped her hands from her face and looked up at him. Her eyes were glistening with unshed tears, an intense shade of blue like the summer sky at noon. He reached down and smoothed a wispy lock of her hair that was falling into her eyes. 'This is stressing you. It is a crazy idea and I'm a crazy man for having dropped you in it.'

She sniffed. 'Now I understand why you did it in the first place. And how very special your mother is to you, so you want to keep it going. It's just I—'

'I would never force you into something you didn't want to do. Ever.'

'I know. And it's because of that I really do want to help you. I also want to be your housemate and help you with Nina. If I tell the truth now, I'll have to go back to my parents' place. Otherwise, it would be incredibly awkward staying here under the scrutiny of your disappointed parents.'

'Now's your chance to back out. Seriously. I'll still be your friend even if you break off our "engagement".'

That brought a watery smile from her. 'I'm in. I'm your fiancée until Wednesday.'

He stepped closer. Took both her hands in his. She looked down to their joined hands and back up to him, alarmed. 'It's only pretend, remember,' he said. 'But we need to be convincing. As you reminded me, I've never kissed you. Engaged people should probably have some knowledge of what it's like to kiss each other.'

Georgia looked up at him, her eyes wide and wary, but still with a trace of smile lingering at the corners of her lips. She usually didn't wear much make-up, but today she'd put something on her eyes that emphasised their blue and the thickness of her dark lashes. Her mouth was slicked with cherry-red gloss and it looked eminently kissable. He'd always found that slight unevenness of her top lip very appealing—now he wanted to know how it felt under his lips, how she tasted, how she felt in his arms.

'Okay, so we kiss,' she said.

'Right,' he said, taken aback by her practical approach.

'Shall I be the first?'

'What do you mea—?'

Before he could finish his question, Georgia had tugged on their linked hands to pull him close and pressed her mouth against his, soft and warm and, to his surprise, hesitant. For all her show of bravado, she was nervous.

Wil wasn't the slightest bit nervous. More like exultant that he had her so close. *Kissing Georgia at last.* He took command of the kiss, being careful to keep his lips on hers tender and undemanding. A shiver of surrender ran through her as she relaxed into the kiss. He tightened his grip on her hands. She parted her lips to welcome his tongue with a little murmur of what he couldn't be sure was pleasure or trepidation. He vowed, with a fierce surge of protectiveness, he would make sure she felt only pleasure from his touch.

Her curves were soft and yielding against his chest. He slid his hands around to grasp her waist and pull her even closer. The wrap skirt of her dress had swung open to the top of her taut, toned thighs and her legs were bare against his. When her tongue met his, tentative at first and then meeting his in a sensual tangle, he was stunned by the sudden and intense shock waves of pleasure that rippled through his body—and his heart.

Her first kiss with Wil. It was so much more than Georgia could ever have imagined. She was almost overwhelmed by excitement. *This isn't real*, she tried to remind herself, but she couldn't think logically when she was so overwhelmed by sensation. This was Wil, familiar, yet, oh, so unfamiliar. His mouth, tasting of coffee and his favourite chocolate cookie. His scent, citrus shower gel with a heady touch of fresh, manly sweat. His hard, perfect male body in such intimate contact with hers.

What had started as a harmless practice kiss had flamed into something else altogether and escalated to a passionate exchange that surprised the heck out of her. Her heart hammered, her body pulsed with want. They'd always had a connection, mental, spiritual, now it was physical. The difference between friend and potential lover. Her heart gave a huge jolt. She broke away from the kiss to catch her breath, to find her balance. If she didn't pull away from him, she'd be dragging him behind the house and pushing him up against the wall.

She came up for air, panting, holding on to her heart. Wil was the same, his eyes dazed and unfocused. He seemed as knocked out as she was by what they had unleashed.

'What happened there?' she gasped.

Wil was drawing in great gulps of air in an effort to steady his voice. 'Eight years of wanting to kiss you? What's your guess?'

'Same,' she managed to choke out. The thought struck her. 'Or was it an act? On your part, I mean. You know, to look authentic.'

'I sure as hell wasn't acting. What about you?'

She shook her head. 'No. It…it was real.'

Georgia looked up at him and, as had happened so many times before, their eyes connected and they laughed. She felt exhilarated, high almost. Her buddy Wil. The best kisser she'd ever kissed.

He planted a firm, hard kiss on her mouth. 'Who knew?' he said, then proceeded to answer his own question. 'That's why I held off from ever kissing you. I suspected it might be like that for us. Did you not wonder why I never did, in those rare times when we were both single?'

'I could as easily ask you the same thing.

A woman doesn't just hang about waiting to be kissed, you know. Not this girl, anyway.'

At that he laughed and pulled her back for another kiss. A kiss that caught her mouth when they were both still laughing, that made it seem an extension of their friendship. Which was so much more powerful than any impulse fuelled purely by desire.

She pressed her body close to his with a moan of impatience. Slid her hands up and under his loose shirt to feel the warm, bare skin of his back. She forgot where she was, why she was there. If she and Wil had been in the middle of George Street in Central Sydney with the world buzzing around her, she wouldn't have cared. *Him*. Wil. And the revelation of how much she wanted him.

But the sound of the door opening made her still. Wil too. She murmured a curse against his mouth, so low only she and Wil could hear it. Pulled away from the kiss. Looked up into his face. Saw the same dazed look of being pulled back into reality too quickly so her feet were scarcely holding her to the ground, still in the dizzying world where it was just her and Wil and their bodies in tune with each other.

They both turned as one towards the front door to the house. Jackie. His mother stood there, holding on to the door frame, as if what she had seen had come as a shock. But she was grinning, a huge grin that lit up her face and made her look ten years younger.

'Sorry to interrupt,' she said, laughter lacing her voice. 'Nina's getting a little grizzly with just old folks for company.' She turned to head back inside, the grin dialled down now to a happy smile. 'But she can wait a little longer for her dad,' she said as she disappeared inside.

Now it was Wil's turn to curse, much more strongly than Georgia ever would.

She fought to get her breath back. 'It's okay,' she said. 'We did leave Nina for longer than we probably should have. They're still strangers to her. If you think about it, that worked out better than we could ever have planned. I suspect your mum is in there telling your dad how happy she is to have witnessed what she witnessed. That all is well with their son and his girl. And that's what this is about, isn't it?'

'It did the trick,' he said. 'But, play-acting aside, I enjoyed it.' His eyes drilled down into hers, dark with desire and something else she couldn't read, asking questions she was incapable of answering.

'Me too,' she said, unable to resist reaching up to give him a quick kiss on his mouth. He snatched her hand and kissed the palm. Even that felt thrilling. Shivers of excitement coursed through her. 'But I'm not sure what we should do about it,' she said.

He grinned. 'Now you consign me to oblivion.'

'What? Oh, yes, I remember. But you've got it wrong. Didn't you say I would consign you to oblivion if I didn't like you kissing me?' She narrowed her eyes, pouted her lips. 'Who said I didn't like it?'

With a triumphant whoop, he drew her back into his arms and kissed her again.

Georgia knew she should be breaking away and talking about keeping the two different types of PDA apart. That otherwise they'd be heading to heartbreak. But all she could think about was that she'd be sharing a bedroom with Wil that night and what the heck was she going to do about it?

CHAPTER NINE

GEORGIA LET WIL take her hand as they headed back into the house. *Holding hands with Wil.* Who knew it would feel so good, his much larger hand enfolding hers, warm and relaxed? It felt so natural and uncontrived, she couldn't imagine ever walking along beside him without holding his hand. But it wasn't real. It was an act, one in which she was willingly colluding.

Already she had started to talk herself out of what had seemed so very real outside—those passionate kisses. Obviously, they were both healthy young people who liked each other and no longer denied they found each other attractive. Of course their first kiss would ignite all sorts of feelings. But her reaction—and she supposed his—was purely physical. A friends-with-benefits scenario could work, if it remained strictly physical. *But that wasn't going to happen.*

Her feelings towards her long-time friend

went beyond the physical. But there was too much in the way, blocking them from proceeding to anything deeper. Give in to a physical fling with Wil and she would lose him for ever. That first kiss aside—that exciting, wonderful, arousing kiss—the way she had handled her attraction to him for so long must still stay in play. Keep him as a hands-off friend or risk him becoming a lost former lover she would mourn? The choice was obvious.

The table in the family room, where morning tea had been set, had been cleared and she could hear Dave rattling around in the kitchen. Jackie was sitting on the sofa with Nina asleep against her chest, her little head with its cap of dark hair so like Wil's resting on her grandmother's shoulder. It made a beautiful picture and warmed Georgia's heart. She itched to sketch them. Although there was no actual blood connection, Jackie and Dave had instantly welcomed Nina as their own. 'Just a little wind bothering her, I think,' Jackie whispered. 'The old patting-the-back trick still works a treat—a good burp and she was fine.'

Wil sat down on the sofa and Georgia sat close to him a little hesitantly. How did he want her to play this from here? He put his arm around her to bring her closer, so close their knees were nudging. She tugged her skirt around her so at least skin wasn't touching skin in a situation that was already way too distracting. Then he took her hand in his again.

Georgia noticed Jackie glance at her hand linked with Wil's and was treated to a smile of warm approval. Her 'all is right with my world' look of contentment made Georgia glad she had agreed to carry on the charade of the engagement. This was a good woman; Georgia was doing a good thing in helping make her happy.

'Wil, I notice Georgia isn't wearing an engagement ring,' Jackie said. 'Have you decided not to get one or…?'

Wil, so obviously taken by surprise, didn't answer for a moment that seemed to stretch on and on. Georgia was just about to jump in with a hastily thought-out explanation when he finally spoke. 'We haven't had a chance to get one yet, Mum. I told you, our engagement is only a very recent thing.'

'That's right,' said Georgia, thinking on the spot. 'Wil…he wanted me to choose my own ring. Not him doing the old-fashioned thing of him buying it without any input from me.'

As poor Toby had done, with the lovely diamond ring he'd bought to surprise her when he'd proposed. She would never forget his heartbreak when she'd said 'no'. She'd realised she didn't love him enough to marry him. But along with her anguish at hurting him had been exultation. The realisation that she didn't have to compromise her own happiness just to make someone else happy had been like a bucket of ice water thrown over her, awakening her from her people-pleasing, 'good old Georgia' ways.

'Right, yes,' said Wil. 'After all, Georgie is the one who'll be wearing it. She can have any ring she wants.'

Georgia cringed inside at his words, though she kept a sweet fake-fiancée smile glued to her face. The thought of Wil buying a ring for another woman made her feel more than a touch uncomfortable. After that kiss, the thought of him even holding hands with anyone else hit her with a painful spasm of jealousy. The last time she'd seen her, Angie had waved an enormous diamond around on her ring finger. At the time, Georgia had thought it was an effort to incite envy, a tribute to Wil's bank account rather than to any kind of loving commitment.

Georgia forced the memories away. She had never given a thought to what kind of engagement ring she might want if the day ever came when she found someone she actually wanted to marry. She had turned down three proposals of marriage from three very nice men she'd been deeply fond of but not enough to commit to a lifetime of togetherness. There had always been something missing, but she didn't know what it was. Intensity perhaps. She wanted to be head over heels in love with the man she married. Nothing less. In some deep, hidden corner of her heart she was beginning to wonder if she would *ever* love anyone like that. *Maybe she didn't have it in her to be a wife.*

'What kind of ring do you like, Georgia?' Jackie asked.

Georgia thought quickly. 'I think a coloured stone.'

'Then a coloured stone is what you shall have,' said Wil, a little too heartily, Georgia thought. But his mother didn't seem to notice the strain in his voice.

'The reason I ask,' said Jackie, 'is that I have my mother's engagement ring. It's dated in style but quite magnificent with a huge emerald and surrounded by diamonds. You could have it remodelled if you think that might suit, or just use some of the stones.'

'Mum, I—' Wil started to protest.

'I know you can well afford to buy Georgia any ring she wants, but it was just a thought. A way to welcome Georgia to the family with a link to the family past.' She looked to Georgia. 'Your choice, of course.'

'Mum, that's what I was going to say. About the family past. Shouldn't Grandma's ring go to Ned? Not…not to me.'

Wil tightened his grip on Georgia's hand without, she thought, realising he did it. Her heart ached at the naked vulnerability on his handsome face. He must at times have felt second-best to their birth son but would never show it. However, both she and his mother had seen it now, breaking through his happy, just-engaged mask.

'Why would that be?' Jackie said. 'I've always said, as I didn't have a daughter, whoever of my sons first got married could have first choice of Grandma's jewellery. Ned is way behind—he isn't even dating anyone. Besides, there are other rings for when his turn comes.'

Wil let go of her hand, put both his hands on his knees as he leaned towards his mother. 'But, Mum—' Georgia could see now what Wil had meant when he'd said he found it difficult to get a word in when his mother was on a roll. He was too respectful to simply barge in and interrupt.

'If you're going to say something about Ned being my birth son and you my adopted son, you can forget about it. You know I consider you equally both my sons, end of story.'

Georgia wanted to hug her. She and Dave had given Wil such unconditional love he had overcome the disadvantages of his youth to be the confident, successful man he was. They obviously had a lot of love to give—extending it immediately to Nina and, she realised, to her. It made her feel doubly bad about deceiving them.

'Mum, thank you,' Wil said, and Georgia could hear the love in his voice too. Thank heaven they had come along when they had in his life.

'So what are your thoughts about the ring?' Jackie said. 'Georgia?'

The vintage emerald ring sounded like just the kind of thing she would love. But she was never likely to lay eyes on it. No emerald rings for platonic pals. By the time Wil's parents got back from Italy, Georgia the fiancée would have shrunk back to being just the friend. She wouldn't dare meet with Jackie and Dave again. They were so protective of Wil, they would assume she had hurt their son. Toby's parents had actually hated her for 'leading their son on'. Right up to the moment Toby had said, 'Will you marry me?' she had planned to say yes. Toby had ended up hating her too.

'Er…it sounds amazing,' she said. 'I guess I… We…need to see it first. Thank you for your very generous offer.'

'My parents were very happily married,' said Jackie. 'So the ring comes with good karma.' Georgia couldn't help but wonder what kind of bad karma this deception would bring with it.

'That's good to hear,' Georgia murmured, not daring to meet Wil's eye.

Wil patted her on her knee as a fiancé might and she had to stop herself from flinching. Not because she didn't like it, but because she did. From never feeling Wil's touch, she now had lost count of the occasions she had revelled in his touch. *That kiss!*

'It's a very generous offer and Georgia and I thank you,' he said.

Georgia couldn't—wouldn't—point out the elephant in the room that no one was acknowledging. Wil actually had already been the first son to get married. But the parents had so obviously not approved of his choice. She, Georgia, was the favoured one. But she was the fake. She wanted to be far away when Wil told them they had broken their engagement.

'I'll make sure you get a chance to see the ring as soon as possible,' Jackie said. 'Now, while we're all here together, there's something else I want to ask you.'

Georgia exchanged a quick glance with Wil. What next to test them? He looked relaxed but there was tension in the way he held his shoulders, the set of his jaw. She still couldn't believe she was sitting here pretending to be engaged to him while fighting as hard as she could to quell the insistent little voice telling her how nice it was to be considered a couple. Her and Wil. Not to be actually engaged. Of course not. That could never work with Wil. But sitting here so close to him. *Belonging* felt very good.

'What's that, Mum?' Wil asked.

'Have you and Georgia thought about Nina's christening?'

Wil was hit from left field with that one, but only Georgia seemed to notice. 'No,' he said. 'You know I'm not particularly religious, but I guess a christening or a naming ceremony might be a good thing.'

Georgia had no opinion on Nina's religious upbringing. As a fake fiancée, she didn't think she should proffer any ideas.

His mother, however, had strong opinions. 'According to her mother's sister, Nina has not been christened into any faith, or even had a naming ceremony. If you don't have any feelings either way, your dad and I would like to see her christened in our denomination as she is the newest member of our family.'

'Sure,' said Wil.

'What do you think, Georgia, as Nina's future stepmother?' asked Jackie.

If her 'engagement' was real, she'd know who she could talk to about her fears of being a good stepmother. Here was Jackie, proving again and again her mother's love for Wil—the child of strangers—whom she had not even met until Wil was thirteen. 'I hadn't really thought,' she said.

Jackie smiled in understanding. 'The word *stepmother* has such bad connotations, doesn't it? Is there ever a non-wicked stepmother in stories? But as his adoptive mother, I genuinely love Wil as my own, and you will come to love Nina too. And she you—the love goes both ways.'

'Of course,' said Georgia, suddenly aware that she could be giving the game away if she didn't show some enthusiasm for her future—though fictional—parenting duties. 'Nina is adorable, such a cute baby.'

'You have a head start with her,' Jackie said.

'What's that?' asked Georgia, genuinely interested.

'You already love Wil, and he loves you.

You two have got a strong love that goes back a long way. Because you love Wil, you'll learn to love and cherish his daughter. She looks so like him, doesn't she?'

Georgia flushed. She felt like such a hypocrite. Wil took her hand again and squeezed it in a good semblance of lovingly. But she noticed he looked straight ahead instead of at her. He felt it too.

'Yes, I can see that,' she said faintly. She hadn't expected this and she was squirming with guilt and discomfort. How lovely Jackie was, to include her in the family from the start. How duplicitous she and Wil were. But it was what Wil thought was best. And she was—had always been—on his side.

'Back to the christening, what are your thoughts, Georgie?' said Wil.

'My mother always says, apart from the spiritual aspect, being christened is important to get into some of the top private schools in Sydney.'

Wil stared at her. 'That's extremely cynical,' he said. 'I don't know that I like it.'

Wil might not have come from wealth, but he had been adopted into it. Then amassed his own fortune. Georgia shrugged. 'Fact of life in posh Sydney circles. You attended a prestigious private boarding school in Melbourne.

Perhaps you'll want the same kind of school for Nina.' Darn. She'd said *you* not *we*. She darted a look at Jackie. Thankfully, she didn't seem to have noticed the slip-up.

'She's right, Wil,' said Jackie.

'I hadn't given a thought to Nina's schooling,' Wil said. 'Getting her from one feed and nappy change to the next is all I've been focusing on. Regarding schools, I…we…will decide what's best for Nina when the time comes.'

'Of course,' said Georgia. By that stage she wouldn't have anything to do with the decision. Except to give an informed schoolteacher opinion to her friend Wil, who she wouldn't see much of as he was so caught up being a single dad. Or not. *No.* She wouldn't let herself think of Wil with a new wife helping him with Nina.

'Mum, if it's important to you to welcome Nina into the family with a ceremony, I'm okay with it.'

'Me too,' said Georgia, as it seemed to be expected of her.

Jackie beamed. She shifted Nina, who had been sleeping soundly through the entire exchange, to her other shoulder. 'We're leaving for Italy on Wednesday. Would it be possible to get the christening organised for the Tuesday?'

'Tuesday?' said Wil, shocked. 'Today is Saturday. How could we—?'

'We've never organised a christening. Can you get it done in that time?' said Georgia.

'Wouldn't it be better to wait for you to come back from Italy to have the ceremony?' said Wil.

'Nina is already seven months old,' said Jackie. 'We don't want to leave it much longer. Besides… I… Well, there's no beating around the bush. I'm feeling well now. But who knows what the future holds for me?'

'Mum,' said Wil, anguished. 'Don't say that. Please.'

'It's a fact of life, son.'

Georgia put her hand comfortingly on his arm, now she was 'allowed' to do that. 'We'll see what we can do, Jackie.'

'If we can organise a christening for Tuesday, we will,' said Wil.

'If you don't mind me putting my oar in, I know the priest at a church in Manly—he used to be in our parish,' said Jackie. 'That's not too far from here. I'll see what he could do about fitting us in for a quick christening. It might be okay on a weekday, if we take whatever time they give us. Not to mention a generous donation on offer.'

'Sure,' said Wil. 'Georgie is on school holidays and my time is my own.'

Georgie actually has illustrations to finish,

'Coming on top of the urgency of the christening, I'd really had enough, much as I love her,' he said.

'I couldn't look at you or I would have laughed out loud when you laid down the law. When you told her in such a controlled voice that we'll get married in our own good time—and that it wouldn't be until after she comes back from Italy.'

'I really had to grit my teeth when she suggested we might consider a destination wedding in Tuscany and that, if we liked, she could set the wheels in motion while she was over there.'

'I had to stop myself getting excited about that one. I mean, if it were real, if we really were getting married. Tuscany.'

'I didn't want to get cranky with her, but I'd had enough. I'm not as good at creating fibs on the spot as I thought I would be.'

'That's actually a good thing, Wil,' she said. 'I'm not a natural-born liar either. It's exhausting.'

'Mum kept us both on the spot,' he said. 'But you played your part so well, Georgie. I'm having another grovelling with gratitude moment.'

Wil threw himself down on one of the upholstered armchairs that were arranged around

Georgia thought, but how could she protest? She had the uncomfortable feeling she was being steamrollered, even if it was for the best of reasons.

'What about your family, Georgia?' said Jackie. 'It will be short notice for them. Do you think they will be able to attend the christening?'

Georgia stared at her, unable to speak. Her throat closed over. 'My family?' she managed to choke out. 'Oh, I…er…don't think so.'

'They may want to see their step-granddaughter christened,' Jackie said.

Step-granddaughter? Of course, they would be Nina's step-grandparents. If this were for real.

Wil came to the rescue. 'We hadn't actually thought that far ahead.'

Georgia had no intention of telling her family anything about the fake engagement. She'd hoped she could keep it confined to Ingleside. This was in serious danger of spiralling out of control.

If her mother thought she was engaged to Wil, she'd cancel a court case to be there and meet his family. Her sisters would be agog. They always teased her that she'd let Wil—who they were convinced was her Mr Right—

get away. Once they knew, half of Sydney would know.

'We only want a very small ceremony, Mum,' said Wil. 'Ideally, just you, Dad, me and Georgie. That's what I want.' Georgia could see him improvising as he went along. 'For one thing, it would be in bad taste to have anything other than to keep it very small and very private when you consider it's so soon after Angie's death. I know we were divorced, but just out of respect. That's my final word.'

'I agree with Wil, of course,' said Georgia. In this case she most certainly did.

Jackie nodded. 'I can see your reasoning behind that decision. Small and private it shall be.'

Georgia looked to Wil and smiled, hoping she was masking her intense relief. He smiled back. Crisis averted.

But Jackie hadn't finished. 'But I'll need to get in touch with your parents anyway, Georgia,' she said. 'After all, we'll all want to pull together to organise the wedding. Have you two set a date?'

CHAPTER TEN

LATER THAT EVENING Wil was alone with Georgia in his bedroom. Not so much a bedroom but a luxurious hotel-like suite with the finest of furnishings in muted neutrals. His mother had pulled out all the stops on the master bedroom when they'd redecorated the house. Wil shut the door firmly behind him and Georgia to ensure their privacy. Nina's room was the next down the corridor; the bedroom his parents were sharing at the other end.

'What a day,' exclaimed Georgia, laughing, whirling around to face him. 'Your mum! She's a darling, but she never stops.'

'Never stops trying to organise my life, you mean,' he said, his tone mildly exasperated yet not masking his love for his mother. 'And now yours.'

'The look on your face when she asked us had we set a wedding date—I nearly cracked up,' said Georgia.

the marble fireplace. In winter, it kept the room toasty warm. Now a ceiling fan flicked overhead to supplement the air conditioning on a steamy summer night. He indicated for Georgia to take the other, tried not to notice the way her wrap skirt slid away from her legs when she sat down. She glanced up, noticed the direction of his eyes, tugged the fabric more modestly around her.

It was the first time they had been alone since the kiss outside on the driveway. There had been lunch with his parents at the house around the pool, then dinner, Nina included, at a waterside restaurant in Manly. Not surprisingly, the Manly trip had also included a drive-by of the proposed church for the christening.

'The highlight for me was when your dad came out of the kitchen with a dishcloth dangling from his hand and told your mum we would decide a date for our wedding when we were good and ready and not before,' said Georgia as she settled into the chair with a delightful wiggle of her bottom. Wil was noticing so many habits and quirks about her that he'd never noticed before. Though he'd admired her back view clad in tight riding breeches on many occasions over the years of their friendship.

Georgia continued. 'Then your dad said

you'd only just found out you're a father and to give the boy some space.'

'Dad's a man of few words, but he keeps his finger on the pulse,' he said.

Georgia drew her dark brows together. 'Do you think he suspects something isn't right? Between us, I mean?'

'No. He lets his sons get on with their lives. He's always there if I need him, I can count on that. Otherwise, he doesn't interfere.'

'Except when he entered you for the reality inventors show without telling you.'

'For which I will always be grateful. At that age, I would never have found the guts to enter it myself. The exposure gave me such a kick-start. I wouldn't be where I am without the contacts it brought.'

'And now you've got all this,' she said with a wave around the room. 'This bedroom is like a six-star hotel.'

But has only come to life with you in it, Wil thought. Her megawatt smile, the brightness of her eyes, the vivid splash of colour from her dress were like a series of lights being switched on to illuminate the stark loneliness of the space.

He got up to fetch a bottle of white wine and two wine glasses and placed them on the low glass coffee table in front of them. Nina's baby monitor was on the mantelpiece. She had been put to bed by her doting grandmother but it would be Wil who would get up to her during the night, if needed.

When his mother had interior designed this room, she had thought of everything. An enormous king-sized bed dressed with fashionable linen and rather too many cushions for his taste, a comfortable sofa, these chairs, a walk-in dressing room, even a small fridge hidden behind custom cabinetry. She'd had the existing bathroom ripped out and replaced with elegant new fittings and marble tiles with underfloor heating. It was a bedroom that a boy in residential care sharing a room with other boys, sleeping in a narrow bed with an envelope-thin mattress and a metal locker for his few possessions, could never have imagined would be his.

Georgia sipped at her wine, looking at him over the rim. 'I know we're having a laugh at your mother's expense, but it's lovely the way she's so excited about it all. If we really were organising a wedding, she'd be a great help.'

'I have to admit, I thought only as far as an engagement. Mum threw me when she asked about a wedding date.'

Georgia leaned forward in her chair. 'And yet, you've been married before.'

He put down his glass, unable to take even a sip of his wine for fear he might gag on it. 'I don't count that as a marriage. More a…a short-term spell in prison.'

Georgia couldn't disguise her gasp. 'Was it that bad?'

'Yep,' he said.

'Are you ready to tell me about it?'

'As you've become so involved in my life, I guess you should know,' he said.

'Only if you want to share,' she said, thoughtful as ever.

How different his life might have been if she hadn't met Toby and he hadn't met Angie and they'd decided to try out where that deeply buried attraction between them might have led to. Too late now. All this talk of engagement rings and weddings made him shudder. He had no plans to re-enter that trap called marriage any time soon. Perhaps never. Besides, looking after Nina took up all his energies. Though having Georgia here to help would make a huge difference. He wouldn't let himself think about how it would be, when she'd leave to go back to school.

'Angie caught me on the rebound,' he said.

Georgia screwed up her face in concentration. 'Who were you dating then? Oh, yes, that nice red-headed physiotherapist.'

'Yeah,' he said.

That wasn't the rebound he was referring to. But he had no intention of telling Georgia that she had been the one he'd lost and, in his loss, he had been vulnerable to a woman like Angie.

At the time, Georgia had seemed so keen on Toby. Wil hadn't actually needed the 'back off from my girlfriend' confrontation with Toby one night when their group had all been out at a pub. Wil had already realised he'd left his move too late, that there'd been no chance then of suggesting he and Georgia step out of the friendship zone and try dating. Not when she was more serious than he'd ever seen her about another guy—and Toby about her. As Georgia had said, their stars had never aligned.

'Where did you actually meet Angie?'

'In a takeaway coffee shop. She'd just been served and she accidentally spilled some coffee on me. I brushed it off, but she insisted on buying me another coffee, even suggested she pay for my dry cleaning.'

'Meet cute,' said Georgia.

He frowned. 'What do you mean?'

'It's a movie term to describe a cute, uncontrived meeting.'

'There was nothing uncontrived about it, I discovered later,' he said grimly. 'That meeting was totally contrived. Angie had been watching me as a hunter watches its prey. She'd seen me on TV, you see. Knew my worth down to the last dollar.'

'I don't mean to defend Angie, Wil. But there might have been more to it than that. You are extraordinarily handsome, you know.'

Dear Georgia, always wanting to be fair. But there had been nothing fair about the way Angie had behaved. 'That's nice of you to say so,' he said.

'So what happened next?'

'She was very attractive, she pursued me, and I allowed myself to be caught.'

'You were quite the player in those days.'

'Perhaps,' he said.

'So how did you end up marrying her so quickly?'

'More wine?' he asked. Georgia held out her glass for a refill. Wil topped up his glass. 'To answer that, I have to go back again to those times of my life I'd rather not remember.'

'Are you sure, Wil?' Her eyes were warm with sympathy. He knew she'd been shaken by hearing about his childhood. But he hadn't told her everything.

'Yes. You should know. Now that you're so caught up with me and Nina.'

He left the wineglass on the table, after all.

He needed to be sober for this. Not to mention clear-headed enough to face the challenge ahead of having Georgia in his bedroom all night.

'Angie reminded me of a girl named Tegan I met in foster care—my last foster home when I had just turned thirteen. Tegan was the same age as me, dainty, blonde and very pretty.'

Georgia smiled knowingly. 'You had a crush on her.'

'I guess I did. I liked her a lot.'

'Hormones kicking in,' she said.

'Unfortunately the foster father had his eye on her too.'

'Oh, Wil, no.' Her smile disappeared like ice thrown onto a fire.

'As a foster kid, I learned the hard way to shut up and make myself compliant. I was very young for my first placements. Apparently I cried and screamed at being shunted into a house with strangers. Regressed to bed-wetting. Tried to run away. Got the label of troublemaker from an early age.'

'Five years old,' Georgia whispered. She raised her hand as if reaching out to comfort him but lowered it. The 'no touching in private' rule was back in place.

'I soon learned that the amiable kids do best in foster care. Yes, sir, no, sir, do as you're told.

Don't get attached to any of the nice foster parents, when you know you won't be staying. When I was younger, I saw stuff I didn't understand. I thought it was bad but I didn't know why. You learn to turn the other way if you see something scary, otherwise you'll be in trouble.'

Georgia snatched her hand to her mouth. 'Were you abused?'

'No, I wasn't. Other boys were, but thankfully not me.'

'Thank heaven.' She breathed out a huge sigh of relief. 'What happened with Tegan?'

'When I realised this guy was grooming Tegan for abuse, I couldn't turn a blind eye. I warned her never to be alone with him, no matter what threats or promises he might make to her. That didn't keep her safe. When Tegan told me what he'd tried to do, I went for the guy. I was nearly as tall then as I am now. And used to defending myself at school. He was taken by surprise and I was angry. I managed to do some serious damage—broke his nose, knocked out a few teeth. That's when I got put into the care home. Got myself some respect from the other boys for beating up a foster parent.'

'But not much from the authorities, I'll bet.'

'None. I never went back into foster care—

no one wanted me, not surprisingly. The foster father didn't press charges. He didn't want to be looked at too closely. So I was spared Children's Court and a spell in a juvenile justice centre.'

'And Tegan?'

'Thankfully, one of the social workers believed me when I told her Tegan was in danger. The guy denied everything, of course. But she was taken out of that house and supposedly sent to somewhere safer. I never saw her again. But I never forgot her.'

'So Angie reminded you of her?'

'Not just in looks. She and Sharyn came from an abusive family situation. Angie had spent time in care too.'

Georgie nodded thoughtfully. 'If you couldn't rescue Tegan, you could rescue Angie.'

He knew his mouth had turned down in a bitter line. It always did when he thought about that disastrous time in his life. 'Not that she really needed rescuing. Her survival technique was manipulation, learned from a very young age. Pretty little Angie could twist the truth like no one I've ever encountered before or since. Though of course she was all charm at first. Until she'd got me on her hook.'

Georgia frowned. 'That begs the question, Wil, why did you marry her?'

'The oldest trick in the book. She told me she was pregnant.'

Georgia sat bolt upright in her chair. 'What?' He could see her going through a mental timeline, realising he didn't mean pregnant with Nina.

'By then I'd started to see beneath the veneer of her pretty ways. Was ready to end it. Angie must have realised that. I'd told her something of my background by then. She knew I would never risk having a child of mine going through what I went through. She gambled that I would marry the mother of my child—no matter what. That's why the hasty marriage at the register office. That's why she didn't want my parents involved in the wedding.'

'You're too honourable to have made any other choice.'

'Too gullible as it turned out,' he said, unable to keep the bitterness from his voice.

'What happened about the baby?'

'Conveniently lost just two weeks after the wedding. I was sympathetic. Sad for her, and sad for me too. I blamed her erratic behaviour that followed on hormone disruption from the miscarriage. Then she told me in one of her screaming fits that she'd never been pregnant at all. The positive pregnancy test kit she'd shown me had come from another woman.'

'Surely not,' Georgia said, visibly shocked. 'How could someone do that?'

Such deception would be beyond someone as thoroughly decent as Georgia. That was the reason he had never told her the truth of his sordid past—fear she would scorn that violent foster kid whose own family hadn't wanted him. That kid masquerading as a wealthy land-owner's son. He'd believed he'd be punching above his weight if he'd tried to get serious with Georgia.

'I left. But she begged me to come back. She knew what strings to pull. I didn't want to admit defeat. Felt I had to give the marriage a fair go. I'd made a commitment. I tried and tried to make it work. But it became more and more toxic.'

'So what happened to make you finally end it?'

Wil angled himself to look directly into her face. 'I'm going to tell you this just the once, Georgie. I don't want to revisit it ever again. I'm only telling you now because I know I can trust you.'

'Of course you can. That goes without say-ing.'

Wil threw his head back, stared at the ceil-ing as he spoke. He didn't want to see pity or condemnation in Georgia's eyes. 'She started to push me further and further. I couldn't do a thing right. She undermined me at every opportunity. Alienated me from my friends. Even tried to do the same with my family.'

Georgia audibly caught her breath. 'Wil, are you telling me she became abusive?'

'A big man and a tiny little woman? Who would believe it? What male wants to admit to being an abused husband?'

'That happens, though, doesn't it? The abused becomes the abuser. Angie was abused and repeated the cycle. The poor woman—in spite of everything you've told me, I feel some pity for her.'

'So did I. At times I could see flashes of the person she could have been. But Angie wouldn't acknowledge she needed help. I actually began to fear I might end up with a knife in my back. I had to admit defeat and walk away for good.'

'How did she take it?'

'Badly, as you can imagine. I paid her off very handsomely when we divorced. But she wouldn't accept my decision. I told her I never wanted to see her again.'

'But it turned out she was pregnant for real.'

'And saw a way to further manipulate and punish me. Stubborn, scheming and plotting revenge.'

Georgia shook her head. 'Keeping your child from you when she knew how much that would hurt you.'

'Until she was ready to strike, according to her sister, Sharyn.'

'What a horror story. Yet for all that, she cared for Nina and looked after herself.'

'Although I only have Sharyn's word on that. Angie abused both alcohol and chemicals—that was part of her problem. Apparently she kept clean through the pregnancy and after the birth. Nina is certainly in excellent health, which points to that being true. I like to believe, for Nina's sake, that perhaps she was Angie's salvation. Who knows? I'll certainly never tell Nina the truth about her mother. Only the good things.'

'I'm reeling, Wil, that you had to go through all this by yourself.'

'Not by myself. There were my parents and Ned and the solace of Five and a Half Mile Creek. I stayed down there as often as I could. Worked remotely. Talked to Mum and Dad. Rode my horse. When I was in Sydney I worked on this house. Another reason you and our other friends didn't see me.'

'I honestly don't know what to say, Wil. You've gone through hell.'

'Now you can see why I was prepared to

fight and even lie to keep Nina. And why I'm so damn grateful to my parents, I lied some more.'

'I just wish I'd been able to help you.'

'You're helping me now, Georgie. That's what counts.' He got up from the chair. Paced up and down in front of the fireplace until he came to a halt in front of her chair. 'Now you know the worst of me, where I came from, what I really am. Do you still want to help?'

CHAPTER ELEVEN

GEORGIA JUMPED UP from her chair to face Wil. 'The worst? What do you mean the worst? More like the best,' she said fiercely. 'Over the last few days you've told me an incredible story of a boy who had a terrible start in life and won through by his strength of character and intelligence to be the amazing man I'm proud to call my friend.' She had to blink away tears, but didn't want him to notice.

He tilted his head. 'You mean that?'

'Of course I mean that. How could you think I wouldn't? I didn't think it could get any more tragic than the five-year-old lost on the beach while his parents drowned. But the thirteen-year-old white knight saving his vulnerable friend from a terrible fate and then being punished for it comes very close. I want to run out of this room and bang on your parents' door and kiss their feet for rescuing you from that dreadful situation. Though in reality, I think you rescued yourself.'

He swallowed hard before he replied, she could see by his Adam's apple. 'That means a lot, Georgie. You and your family are so... north-shore respectable, I suppose is the word for it. I was concerned you would think less of me because of my past.'

'Why? That you were somehow not worthy because of the dreadful childhood you suffered through no fault of your own? Because adults let you down? I hate your aunt, by the way. I hope you never see her.'

'No chance of that, even if I'd wanted to. She moved house and left no forwarding address.' He couldn't hide the pain of rejection from his voice, after all that time.

'I hope she came to a horrible end,' she said with narrowed eyes and a melodramatic tone.

He laughed and it warmed her heart to hear it. 'Loyal Georgie,' he said.

'To think what you've made of yourself since that start. I'm so proud of you, Wil.'

'Thank you,' he said simply.

She ached for him—it literally felt as though she had a pain in her chest—for all he'd gone through as a kid. 'How strong you must be to have won through all that. And then to have to cope with that terrible marriage.'

'I guess,' he said gruffly.

She looked up at him. 'I don't give a flying fig about the "no touching" rule right now, Wil. I have to hug you.' She put her arms around him. He felt so good, warm and hard and so utterly male. He tightened his arms around her and held her close. For what seemed like a long time but probably wasn't even minutes, she stood in the circle of his arms, willing all his past pain away. Finally she murmured against his shoulder, 'If your friends had known what you were going through in your marriage, you know we would have rallied around you. Tried to intervene.'

'It wouldn't have done any good. I got myself into the mess and I had to get myself out of it. Besides, you would have been the worst person to have offered help.'

She pulled away, still within the circle of his arms. 'Why was that, Wil?'

'I told you. Angie didn't believe we were platonic friends. I don't know how many times she accused me of, as she said, having "the hots" for you.'

'Funny, Toby said the same thing.'

'You know he warned me off you?'

'I didn't know, but I'm not surprised,' she said. 'He was possessive.'

'He cared for you.'

'He did.'

'What went wrong? Did he cheat on you?'

'No!' Georgia laid her cheek back against his shoulder. It was easier, somehow, to talk about this intensely personal stuff without looking into his face. 'I broke his heart.'

'You told me Toby was "The One", that you were going to marry him.' There was a harsh edge to Wil's voice that she didn't understand.

'I thought I wanted to marry him. He was so nice, good-looking, we had a lot in common, got on well, he made me laugh. We talked about moving in together, but something held me back.'

'The fact that you're the marrying kind?'

'Probably. I'm a romantic, as you know. I wanted the big wedding with all the frills, one day. The head-over-heels-in-love thing.'

'Toby was that,' he said. 'Head over heels, I mean.'

'I know, and I did love him. But in hindsight, I didn't love him enough. Everything pointed to us getting married and I went along with it, thinking it was what I wanted. I knew from all the hints and allusions from our families and friends that he was gearing up to propose.'

'Just as you'd hoped,' Wil said.

'Yes. Though I had a dream one night that

the two of us were waiting on North Sydney station to catch a train. When the train came, he got on the train we were meant to be on but I turned around and got on a different train on the other side of the platform. He looked back from his train to see where I was, as I was meant to be with him. But I was on the other one, behind closed doors, looking out of the window at him as my train drew away in the opposite direction. I woke up shaking and in tears.'

'That dream was telling you something.'

'But I didn't listen to it. Then when Toby did propose, on his knees in the most romantic way I could have wished for, I opened my mouth to say "yes" but "no" came out instead.'

'Ouch. For Toby, I mean.'

'He thought I was joking at first, but I wasn't. I just knew I couldn't marry him. That I loved him but not enough to want to spend my life with him.'

'Let me guess,' said Wil. 'Toby wasn't happy about your decision.'

She looked up at him again. 'You could say that. Needless to say, he ended up hating me. His family hated me. Some of my friends took his side and didn't have nice things to say about me either. And no more golf games between the potential fathers-in-law.'

'Better that happened before you married him than after.'

'So my family said. My mother works in the family law court. She said I did absolutely the right thing. She sees the results of the wrong decisions in court all the time.'

Wil looked down at her. 'Poor Georgie,' he said. He traced a line from her cheekbone to the corner of her mouth.

She stilled. Their gazes connected for a long time. Then he kissed her. He pulled her close and she kissed him back. The kiss escalated quickly from a tender affirmation to a passionate hungry exchange. Wil hadn't shaved since the morning and Georgia found the scrape of his beard unbearably exciting against her skin, his scent familiar and exhilarating. When Wil slid his hands down the sides of her breasts, her nipples hardened and she ached for him to touch her, stroke her and go so much further than kissing. When his hands slid down to cup her bottom, and she began to push her body insistently against him, she pulled away.

'Not a good idea,' she said, panting and trying to get her breath back. Not to be kissing like this, alone with him in his bedroom with that big bed beckoning.

He turned his head from side to side in disbelieving amazement. 'All those years, holding back on kissing you. Now *this*. Who knew how mind-blowing it would be? You know what this means?' He pushed a curl gone frizzy with humidity away from her forehead.

'What does it mean?

'We'd be sensational together in bed.'

'Wil!'

'It's true. You feel it too, don't you?'

Her heartbeat had started to slow down from the kiss. Now it started hammering again and a shudder of anticipation went through her. 'We'd better stop that line of conversation right there.'

'Practical Georgie,' he said, huskily.

'Cautious Georgie who knows this can't lead anywhere but heartbreak,' she said. 'Friends with benefits can't work. Not for people like me, anyway. Sex has to be part of an ongoing relationship, one I think can go somewhere, even if it ends up not to be that way.'

He groaned. 'You're right, as usual.'

'What we have as friends is not worth risking.'

'Not even for mind-blowing sex?'

Georgia flushed at the very thought of it. Moved a step closer to stand under the breeze generated by the ceiling fan. If just kissing Wil could make her feel like this, what would making love with him be like? 'I'm fanning myself at the thought. But you know it wouldn't work.'

That big, empty bed with all those cushions loomed in the room. If she took him by the hand and led him over, would he follow? She clenched her hand into a fist to stop herself from even contemplating it.

'I know,' he said slowly, with what seemed like genuine regret. 'You're right. We should keep that "no touching" rule in place unless required for purposes of enhancing the illusion that we're engaged.'

She hesitated before she replied. 'A few times today, especially when it came to Tuscany, I found myself wondering what it might be like to be actually engaged to you and then—'

His face tightened. 'I'm sorry, Georgie, I can't see myself getting married again. And I know you too well to believe you would settle for anything less than wholehearted commitment.'

'You misunderstood,' she said. She schooled her face to ignore that unreasonable stab of hurt at the thought he could marry a woman like Angie but would never have considered her. *Just friends*, she reminded herself yet again. 'I was going to say that I don't let myself think any further along those lines. Perhaps if we'd acted on…on whatever it is that makes our kisses so mind-blowing several years ago, we might have had a chance. But not now.' She paused, trying to summon up the right words.

She turned away from him. Picked up the baby monitor from the mantelpiece and put it hastily back down as it emitted a blast of static. 'Back then, there wasn't Nina. It's not just about us any more. You don't want to marry again. You've made that clear. I do want to get married and have a family some day. That means if we did have a fling for a while, or a "friendship with benefits" thing, it would be a dead end for me.'

'I'm not sure where you're going.'

'Where would that leave Nina when I left? Crying for me like she cried for her mum? I don't want to be responsible for adding further trauma to that precious little girl's life.'

'Yeah. I get that.'

'Do you? Because I'd be crying too, having to leave her. I might be glad to see the last of you because it didn't work out. Not so Nina. It's too easy to get attached to children. Like the kids I teach and have to say goodbye to at the end of the school year. If I allowed myself to get attached to them, I'd be an emotional wreck.'

'But—'

'You'll have to keep that in mind when you start seeing other women. Think about how any relationships you have could affect Nina.' It killed her to think of him with another woman. But she'd had to get used to that over the years. What was different now?

'I have no plans to see other women,' he said bluntly.

'You will sooner or later,' she said, forcing her words to be even and emotionless. 'And I look forward to playing some ongoing role in Nina's life, maybe like a surrogate aunty.'

Wil paused for a long moment. Georgia thought he had never looked more handsome, his hair all ruffled from her hands running through it, his eyes dark and thoughtful, the sexy shadow of his beard. 'Our stars never aligned, did they?' he said eventually.

'And it looks like they never will,' she said, unable to keep a note of sadness and regret from her voice.

She leaned down to pick up her glass of wine, took a sip, but then put it back down. 'Not a good idea at this time of night. I've had enough.'

She made a show of yawning, putting her

hand over her mouth. In truth, she wasn't tired at all. Not after that kiss. Her body was throbbing with want for him. *We'd be sensational together in bed.*

She could happily make love to Wil all night and not sleep a wink. But she valued their friendship too much to throw it away for a physical thrill that could go nowhere.

He placed his hands on her shoulders so she had to look up at him. 'Georgie, I'm not going to sleep in here tonight. Before, it would have been okay for me to sleep here. Like we did in the horse trailer. But not any more. All day I've been wondering what it might be like to unfasten your dress and watch it slide off your body.'

She gasped. 'Oh.'

'I've been wondering what underwear you have on.'

She cleared her throat. 'Black lace,' she choked out.

He groaned, dropped his hands from her shoulders, stepped back. 'You weren't meant to answer that question, Georgie. Now I'll be in torment all night.'

She screwed up her face. 'Sorry. But I like wearing nice underwear. French lace by preference.'

He groaned again. 'I had you down for simple and white. Which has its own charms, of course.'

Maybe she'd had one glass of wine too many. But she was a little tired of being underestimated by Wil. He thought she wore white granny panties and a sturdy white bra? She was a schoolteacher, not a nun.

'But not quite the same as black lace?' she said, very sweetly.

'That does it.' He kissed her hard and swiftly on her mouth. 'I cannot be in this room with you, imagining you in that underwear.'

'But I don't sleep in my underwear.'

'What do you—?' He put his hand up. 'Don't answer that question.' He searched her face with a quizzical look. 'Georgie, I didn't imagine you could be such a tease.'

She wound her arms around his neck. 'There's a lot you don't know about me, Wil Hudson.' *Never underestimate a girl next door*, she thought.

She kissed him briefly, flicking her tongue between his lips, then stepped back from temptation. 'I don't want to boot you out of your bedroom. That doesn't seem right. The sofa is yours.'

'There's a sofa in Nina's nursery. I slept there the first night. I'm going to head in there now. My parents wouldn't be surprised to find me there in the morning. I'll probably have to get up with her during the night anyway and wouldn't want to disturb you.'

'That's our cover story,' she said. 'I'll back you all the way.' She reached up and kissed him chastely on the cheek. 'Goodnight, Wil.'

CHAPTER TWELVE

WHEN GEORGIA WOKE up on Wednesday morning, it was to the vastness of Wil's empty bedroom. The room was still and quiet, save for the chorus of kookaburras outside. Yet Wil's presence seemed to linger, in the shape of his body moulded in the chair where he most often sat, in the scent of the soap in his bathroom, in the starkly simple black-and-white artworks by a coveted Sydney artist he'd chosen for the walls. For the past four nights he had kept up the pretence of sleeping in his room with his 'fiancée', while in reality sleeping on the sofa in Nina's nursery.

She had offered to take his place but he'd refused. 'I got you into this situation, Georgie, the least I can offer you is a comfortable bed,' he'd said.

There'd been no more kissing, touching or flirting when they'd been alone together. At her request. Back to no touching. *Just friends.*

It was simply too difficult to deal with the sensations and emotions physical contact aroused. And they'd kept the public displays of affection muted in front of Jackie and Dave. Even if they'd been engaged for real, she and Wil had agreed, they wouldn't be getting passionate in front of his parents anyway.

It was still very early but Jackie and Dave had left with Wil while it was still dark. They were booked on a crack-of-dawn flight to Italy from Sydney's Kingsford Smith airport. A sleepy Nina had been bundled into her car seat to go with her father and grandparents on the trip out to the airport. Her grandparents had wanted to enjoy the company of their newly discovered baby granddaughter for as long as possible.

Georgia had been invited to go with them in Wil's car, but she'd demurred. Instead she'd waved them off and then crawled back into bed. She'd thought it important that the family spend some time alone together without the fake fiancée present. Now, more than ever, she realised how very important his parents were to Wil. She'd never got around to kissing their feet, but the sentiment was still there. If Wil ever did marry again, Jackie and Dave would make marvellous parents-in-law. *But not for her.*

Ned was important to Wil too. She'd finally met Wil's older brother on Tuesday at Nina's christening. Ned and his cousin Erin, also a farmer, had flown up from Albury to be godfather and godmother. Ned was like his father with the same colouring and broad shoulders but with more of his mother's energy. Afterwards, at the christening lunch at a beachside restaurant in Manly, Georgia had enjoyed talking horses with him and Erin and heard more about Five and a Half Mile Creek. She'd felt a curious sense of loss as she'd realised she would most likely never get the chance to visit the historic property. Now she knew why Wil had kept her from visiting: she might have discovered the secrets of his childhood he had so successfully kept hidden from his Sydney friends.

The christening had gone off like a charm—friendly, intimate and with Nina on her best baby behaviour. The only thing Georgia had felt uncomfortable about was Jackie's insistence that she hold Nina through most of the ceremony. There had been constant well-meant comments on how quickly Nina had taken to her stepmother-to-be. She knew Nina was too young to understand, but she'd felt as if she were deceiving her too.

On the Monday, Jackie had insisted on taking her on a 'girlie' shopping trip to the posh shops in Mosman to buy her a new dress and hat for the christening. Never had Georgia felt more guilty about the fake engagement than when she'd had to gracefully accept the beautiful, flowing tea dress in a gorgeous muted floral in shades of orange, pink and cream and an elegant wide-brimmed cream straw hat. She'd never be able to wear the outfit again, of course. It was finery bought for a future daughter-in-law, not a fraudulent fiancée.

She got out of bed, slipped on her wrap and padded down the corridor, the marble floor cool beneath her bare feet. The door to the room that would now be hers was open, and she popped her head around it. The room was stylishly decorated in up-to-date shades of duck-egg blue and white. The bed had been stripped and the en suite bathroom cleared of towels. Wil had told her the housekeeper would get the room ready for her to move into tonight. She was glad. It was too unsettling to continue to sleep in Wil's bed.

Instead of drowsing off, she'd spent way too much time wondering what it would be like if Wil were between the linen sheets with her. *Wishing* he were there with her. Putting her hand on the pillow and fantasising his dark head lay there beside hers. Who could blame

her for such imaginings, after those passionate kisses? And his seductive talk of mind-
blowing sex? She had no doubt making love
with Wil would indeed be mind-blowing and
memorable. And she had to stop wishing she
could challenge him to prove it.

Now, in the kitchen, even the splash of
the water pouring from the tap into a glass
sounded loud in the silent stillness of the
house. It seemed so empty without the visitors.
Quiet without Nina. Most of all, it was lonely
without Wil. She missed him, even though
he'd be back home within a few hours. She
put away the three coffee cups she had found
washed and drained on the sink. Then stood
looking at the window over the pool and to the
view of the sea, at a loss of what to do.

It was her first day as a former fake fiancée.
She was now back to officially being Wil's
housemate and friend. She didn't know when
he intended to tell his family that their 'engagement' was off. That was up to him. He'd
got them into this mess and he could extricate
them from it as gracefully as was possible.

The day was forecast to be a scorcher. She
thought about a swim. The family—her included—had spent quite some time around the
pool during their visit. No, she knew what she

wanted to do in the relative cool of the morning. Ride Sultan.

She went back to Wil's room and moved her stuff into 'her' room, which took all of a few minutes, got into her riding gear and headed on down to the stables.

The stable hand Wil employed was there to help her saddle up. So was the ginger cat, who wound himself around her legs and demanded attention. Georgia normally wouldn't choose to ride by herself. But she knew she wouldn't be alone on the bushland trails that adjoined Wil's property. She wouldn't be the only horse lover with the idea of getting out early before the heat of the day set in.

Sultan whickered to her as she approached him in his stable. Whether he was pleased to see her or the carrot she had for him, she didn't know or care. He was a magnificent boy and she told him so as he munched messily on his treat. She'd ridden him on Sunday, putting him through his paces on the sand arena under Wil's watchful eye. Despite his haughty, aristocratic good looks, Sultan had a sweet nature and was impeccably well trained. She'd felt immediately at home on his back. 'He's perfect for you,' Wil had said. 'Ride him whenever you want.'

Once in the saddle, Georgia urged the horse

forward with a nudge of her heels. She couldn't imagine a better place to live than here. Lucky, lucky Wil. And lucky her to be sharing it with him for the next two weeks.

From where he stood outside the stables, with Nina in her stroller, Wil watched as Georgia cantered Sultan up the final stretch of the trail and slowed him to a walk as they approached the gate to his property. She reached down to pat Sultan on the neck and Wil knew she was thanking the horse for the ride. Ever since he had first known her, she had always thanked her mount. She loved and respected horses as much as he did. Even if she hadn't left a note in the family room telling him where she'd gone, he'd known she would have gravitated to the stables.

He had always admired how Georgia looked on horseback. She looked particularly good on his big gelding, horse and rider well matched in terms of skill and temperament. As she neared the stable, she dismounted in one graceful, fluid movement and led Sultan by his bridle towards the bay. She handed him to his very competent stable hand, who would wash Sultan down, feed him, rug him in a summer sheet and turn him out to pasture.

As he had done so many times over the

years, Wil admired how hot Georgia looked in form-fitting cream breeches, shiny high black boots and a plain white polo-style shirt. It was a sexier look than the skimpiest of provocative dresses. Although Georgia had certainly looked beautiful in the dress she'd worn to the christening—elegant and very feminine. She'd been more of a tomboy when he had first known her and he'd rarely seen her out of jeans and riding gear. He liked both her looks. And had spent a disproportionate amount of time wondering what she actually did wear to bed.

Now she took off her protective helmet and shook her hair free. It fell around her shoulders, glossy in the morning sun. Her face was flushed with a fine sheen of healthy perspiration, her eyes shining with the exhilaration that came after an energetic and enjoyable ride. She looked up and caught his eye. He was treated to the full radiance of her smile.

'Wil,' she said, making the sound of his name like a caress. 'You're back. And Nina too.' She put down her helmet and walked towards him. He went to hug her and then remembered he shouldn't. That the 'no touching' rule was back in place. 'Not a good idea,' she said. 'Besides, I'm sticky—it's getting really hot.'

She squatted down to Nina's level in her

buggy. 'Good morning, Miss Nina. Did you have a fun trip to the airport? Did Daddy show you some planes taking off?'

Nina chortled and made baby noises that sounded happy, waving her little arms around. His daughter seemed excited to see Georgia. But that equally might have been excitement at seeing the horse or the ginger cat that had appeared at the sound of Georgia's voice.

'She was fascinated by everything at the airport,' he said. 'Looking around her, taking everything in, not in the slightest bit intimidated by the noise and the activity.'

'You might enjoy travelling, Nina, like your nana and granddad,' Georgia said to Nina. He liked the way she spoke to her, not using baby talk and over-the-top endearments. 'Don't worry, you'll see them again before too long. In the meantime, Daddy and I will do our best to keep you entertained.'

She straightened up to face him. 'Sultan was magnificent,' she said. 'We had a really good trail ride. Your stable hand gave me some advice on which way to go. I met one of your neighbours on the trail and asked him could we ride on the beaches anywhere around here. He said not any more, which is a shame.'

He? Wil felt a surge of jealousy at the thought of Georgia chatting with some good-looking guy on horseback. She was *his*. Jealousy was something new to him when it came to Georgia, born after he'd held her in his arms and kissed her. He dismissed the thought as irrational. She was *his* as in *his friend*. And that didn't preclude her from meeting another guy, dating another guy, even marrying another guy when she found her head-over-heels person who would give her the love and commitment she craved. When that time came he would have to grit his teeth and— He scowled as though a cloud had scudded overhead and blocked the sunlight from the glorious day.

'You okay, Wil?' Georgia said, head tilted.

'Absolutely fine,' he said. 'Thinking about breakfast. I'm hungry. Have you eaten?'

'No,' she said. 'What about Nina?'

'She enjoyed a hearty meal of puréed oatmeal and peach.'

'Nice breakfast. I could do breakfast for us both if you'd like,' she said. 'Maybe a grown-up version of Nina's—muesli and yogurt with fruit? Eggs?'

'I'll gladly accept that offer. You know I'm not much of a cook.' He ate out or ordered in all but the most basic of meals.

He had assumed they would have meals together while they were living under the same roof. Maybe platonic housemates didn't do that. He'd never shared his living space with a housemate to know what behaviour was expected. After being in residential care and then boarding school, he liked his privacy and would pay to maintain it. Georgia, however, could invade his privacy all she liked.

He made his voice sound casual, nonchalant. 'The neighbour you spoke to. Who was he?'

'I didn't get his name. An older man. Very pleasant. On a handsome chestnut stock horse. He told me this whole area had been rezoned and was up for massive redevelopment.' The older guy didn't sound like someone he needed to worry about. Georgia had been more interested in his horse.

'That's true,' he said. 'But I won't be breaking my land up into housing plots. I like it just the way it is.' This property had already experienced a huge increase in value, which was gratifying. Building wealth was important to him, not just for the comforts, but for the security it brought with it. Even though he never had to work again if he didn't want to.

'That's a relief to hear,' she said. 'Your place is heaven, Wil. You must never want to leave it.'

'When I move some of the work operations home, I won't have to,' he said. 'However, I'll still have to travel and hold client meetings in the city office. That's when I'll have to seriously consider employing a nanny.'

'In the meantime you and Nina have me to help,' she said. 'You know, when I was out riding, I was wishing you were with me on Calypso. I realised we were only able to ride together on Sunday because your parents had Nina. We'll have to ride on our own as one of us will have to be looking after Nina.'

'I realised that too,' he said. 'This has really been a crash course in parenting for me, and I'm not anywhere through it yet. Having you here is such a help.'

'As I said, I'm no baby expert. But we can muddle through together like real parents have to learn to, I guess.' *Parents.* Nina only had one parent. Georgia was—what had she called herself?—a *surrogate aunt.*

'When she's older, Nina can ride out with us.' Georgia paused. 'That is, if I'm still coming to visit.'

Her words left so much unspoken. Such as by then she might have a family of her own, and no time or inclination to ride with her old friend. Or a husband like Toby who wouldn't appreciate their friendship.

And him? No action on his part would stop her from visiting him here. He point blank wouldn't get involved with a woman who couldn't deal with his friendship with Georgia. No other woman could be as important to him as Georgia. The realisation hit him with the force of a rearing stallion kicking him in the chest. He didn't want another woman. He wanted Georgia. He cared for her. *There could be no other woman for him.*

'I hope you'll always be coming to visit,' he managed to choke out.

'I hope so too.' She smiled but it was a dimmer version of the high-wattage Georgia smile. Did that sadness in her eyes mean she was envisaging a future that didn't include him in it, even as a friend? *He couldn't bear that.*

Wil cleared his throat. His thoughts were twisting around in a vortex. 'What are your plans for today?' he said casually, as a housemate might.

'After breakfast I really have to catch up on some work. It's been wonderful having your parents here and all the excitement of the christening. But I want to enjoy finishing the illustrations, not rushing them so they become a chore.'

'What's your first book about?' he asked, genuinely interested.

'It's a picture book for very young children, early readers. About a little pink tree frog living in the Queensland rainforest where all the other tree frogs are green.'

'That sounds fun,' he said. 'Cute. I like frogs.'

'It's got a message about ecology, but mainly about friendship and inclusion. And yes, it is fun. I wrote it in rhyming verse. The language is quite rhythmical and I hope kids might clap along to it.'

'I'm sure it's brilliant. You created it. That's guarantee enough. Of course, I'll buy a copy for Nina and ask you to sign it.'

She beamed, the full wattage Georgia smile. 'It will be my pleasure to give you one of my advance copies for Nina.'

'You know you said you were proud of me? Let me return the compliment. I'm really proud of you, Georgie. I don't know much about publishing but I know it's a real achievement to have a book published that you've both written and illustrated.'

'Thank you,' she said, looking pleased.

The cat had come to sit by the buggy, much to Nina's delight. It kept a safe distance from Nina's grabby little hands.

'What's the story you're working on now?' Wil asked Georgia.

'A companion book about a lizard. Don't laugh. It's a very cute lizard.'

'Why would I laugh?' he said. 'I'm agog

with admiration at your talent. Do you see your books as a possible future career?'

'It's my dream. I have so many more ideas bursting to see the light. Which is why I'd like to sit down with you over breakfast and plan just how we're going to manage our time between our respective work and caring for Nina while I'm staying here. I have to earn my rent and horse-riding as per our agreement. But I also have to have some uninterrupted time for work.'

'You mean draw up a roster? Day to day, hour to hour?'

'That's not a bad idea,' she said. 'But can we make it flexible enough, not just to account for a baby's unpredictable behaviour, but also so we can enjoy this good weather in your spectacular home? The house that isn't just a house but, as you said, our own private resort.'

'I want to do whatever makes you happy,' he said. 'And Nina.' He meant that to the core of his soul—and he wasn't referring to the roster.

'And you too, Wil,' she said.

He knew exactly what would make him happy about having Georgia in his house. The schedule would include provision for very adult and pleasurable recreational activities for him and Georgia to enjoy. All when his sweet daughter was asleep.

Now was perhaps not the time to discuss those activities in detail with her. A change in the nature of their relationship. It was not the type of conversation that could easily be scheduled. Push her for more than she was ready to give and he could lose her from his life altogether.

CHAPTER THIRTEEN

MID-MORNING, ONE WEEK LATER, Georgia sat cross-legged on the floor in Wil's family room, close to Nina, who was on her padded pink play mat surrounded by toys. The baby's already extensive collection had been added to by her doting and generous grandparents. She was playing gleefully with a soft toy hammer that sounded snatches of music when she gripped it to bang on her rainbow-coloured plush building blocks. Nina's play time with the hammer was limited as the sound eventually drove adults crazy. Right now it was making Georgia laugh. And when Georgia laughed, Nina responded with her utterly adorable baby chuckle.

While Nina was playing, Georgia was sketching her favourite new subject—Nina. She'd filled page after page, capturing moments with Nina with her cap of dark hair, ever-changing expressions, sweet little feet and hands. Nina awake, Nina asleep, Nina laughing. Even in the two weeks since she'd first met her, Wil's daughter had changed and grown. Georgia found it fascinating to observe. Felt proud of Nina's every little milestone achieved. She knew all the milestones to expect, as Wil was an expert from his internet parenting research. He could quote them verbatim.

Georgia put down her pencil and had one of the conversations she so enjoyed with Nina, with her speaking in full sentences and Nina replying with babble that sounded like speech but didn't yet make sense.

Accepting Wil's invitation had been such a good move. Georgia couldn't remember when she had felt happier. She had the run of Wil's fabulous house and grounds. She was well ahead on her book illustrations and inspired daily by the beautiful surroundings of Wil's property and the adjacent bushland.

Then there was Wil.

And the bittersweet edge to her happiness.

She'd known Wil for eight years—minus the two when he'd been off-limits to her—and thought she'd known him well. She'd liked him a lot. Respected him. Laughed with him. Thought he was a good person—one of the best. All the while fighting her attraction to him. Then when they'd reconnected, he'd shared with her the secrets in his past that had shaped him, and she'd understood him on a deeper level.

But *this*. Living with him day to day. This was getting to know him on a whole new level. Discovering his strengths, his habits and quirks. All endearing in their own way—because they were particular to Wil. She loved being so close to him, sharing with him the everyday life of a newly fledged single dad getting to know and care for his daughter.

She appreciated how considerate he was to both her and Nina. Admired how he treated his staff with respect. Discovered that they were both morning people. Found he always picked the 'twist' when they watched crime shows on television but didn't ruin it for her, just gloated afterwards that he'd been right. Noticed how he poured her favourite drink without her ever having to ask him. Wondered why he picked out every piece of red pepper from his salad or pasta sauce. Recognised he got 'hangry' if he went too long without food. Noticed he walked along the beach with her and Nina, but never went in the surf. Speculated on why he never, ever rinsed out his coffee cup so stains didn't set on the expensive Italian porcelain. Smiled that he didn't care if he wore odd socks.

She'd got to know him so much better.

And to care for him way too much.

At the sound of the sliding door to the back deck, she looked up. And dropped her sketchbook. The pages splayed open, pencil strokes and shading possibly smudged. But she didn't even look down at the book, let alone do anything to protect her precious work. Her entire attention was focused on Wil. Her heart started to hammer.

Wil was clad in nothing but his black swim shorts, his body slick with water, his hair damp to his head. He had a black-and-white-striped towel slung around his shoulders but it did nothing to disguise the power of his muscular arms and chest, the defined hardness of his six-pack, his long strong legs. *Turn around so I can admire your gorgeous butt,* she silently willed him. But was glad when he didn't. She already felt light-headed with desire. Too giddy to be able to get up from the floor. Get turned on at the sight of Wil's back view and she very well might faint from lack of oxygen.

As a man he was perfect, she thought. Not just his body. His heart, his soul, his mind. Well, nobody was perfect—not even Wil. She settled on perfectly imperfect.

'Good swim?' she asked, managing to make her voice sound halfway normal.

'Awesome,' he said.

'You were churning through the water.' She'd been keeping an eye on him through the glass doors as he did laps. He didn't like to swim alone.

'I'll head for the shower,' he said.

I'll join you there. She said it in her head. Of course she didn't dare say the provocative words out loud. No matter how much she might want to. As he headed towards the bedroom wing, she tried to force her heart-rate back to normal with a series of deep, calming breaths.

She couldn't endure this for much longer. Living with him. Wanting him. *Falling in love with him.*

She couldn't deny it to herself any longer. Her feelings went way beyond friendship. But it was futile to allow them to flourish. Nothing had changed. There was no hope that it would. She was happy here, but it was a half-life. Studiously playing at being *just friends* when the more time she spent with him, the more she knew she wanted so much more. Stay in this house for too much longer and she might one day do something foolish like follow him to the shower, slip off her shorts and cotton broderie anglaise top and join him there, let him strip her of her pink lace underwear, then wind her arms around his neck, press her naked body against his, together under the stream of water and—

The direction of her thoughts made her flush all the way down her neck. Besides, she couldn't join Wil in the shower for so many reasons. Not the least of which, she was looking after Nina. *Nina.* That was another issue.

She glanced over at where Nina was lying on her tummy on her mat, reaching out for her hammer. 'What's my darling little girl doing? That hammer is—' She stopped herself, aghast.

What had she said? Slip of the tongue. Nina wasn't *her* little girl. She buried her face in her hands when she realised something else she'd been denying—she was falling in love with Nina too. Risking her heart getting broken, not once, but twice. *How had she allowed this to happen?* All those years of resisting her attraction to Wil and now this.

With hands that weren't quite steady, she put her sketchbook back into order and tucked it under a cushion on the settee. She didn't want Wil to see her sketches of Nina just yet. They were too rough and unfinished.

By the time Wil returned to the room, thankfully her flush had faded and her heart rate was approaching normal. Only for it to accelerate at the sight of him in loose, white cotton drawstring trousers and a white vest that emphasised his muscles, played up his tanned skin and dark hair. His hair was still damp from the shower he had taken, unfortunately, alone.

She got up from the floor to greet him. Unaware of her blatant ogling, he headed for the kitchen, brought her back a tall glass of fizzy mineral water packed with ice and lime wedges. 'Just what I needed,' she said, taking it from him. She sat down on the sofa, making doubly sure the sketchbook was concealed.

'I know,' he said, his smile unleashing that devastating dimple. 'You look a little flushed. Do I need to adjust the air conditioning?'

'Er…no. I've been playing with Nina.' She made a show of pushing her hair back from her face to avoid meeting his gaze, for fear he might read the out-of-bounds thoughts she'd been having about him.

He took his favourite place on the other sofa, put his frosted iced tea on the coffee table, looked dotingly over at his mini-me daughter. 'Time to take the musical hammer away, perhaps?'

'She's tossed it out of reach. Let's hope she's tired of it.'

'No chance of an adult conversation over the sound of that thing.'

Georgia resettled herself on the sofa. 'Wil, about that. Conversation, I mean. I need to talk to you. School goes back in ten days. That means I'll be moving back to my parents' place. I think you need to start looking for a nanny. I'll be able to help you interview so we…you get the right one.'

Georgia had rarely seen Wil stuck for words. Now he seemed flabbergasted. 'This is from left field.'

'We always knew I'd only be here for the holidays,' she said gently.

'I… I can't bear to think of you leaving here. I don't want that. Nina doesn't want that.'

Georgia didn't want that. But it would be too painful to stay, continuing the act that she only cared for him as a friend, whereas she was on the edge of falling in love with him. How would she endure it if—when—he started to date again? What would she do if he brought a woman home to his bedroom? To overstay her time here could end in disaster—and the complete loss of her friendship with Wil.

'The time has gone so quickly,' he said. 'Don't be in a rush to go. Do you like it here?'

'I love it. In fact, I can't imagine a better place to live anywhere.'

'So why can't you stay?'

'What do you mean?'

'The living arrangements are working well, aren't they?'

'Yes,' she said. *Except for all the sleepless nights when I lie awake wishing I were in your bedroom with you.*

'Then why not stay on as my housemate? Indefinitely, I mean.'

Georgia hadn't been hoping for anything more romantic. Of course she hadn't. Wil had made it very clear he couldn't promise commitment. She had made it clear that both for her and Nina's sakes, she couldn't settle for anything less. She was cranky at herself for feeling so deflated. Hadn't she herself pointed out that their stars would never align?

'It wouldn't work, Wil. I teach at North Sydney. It's quite a long trek from here in peak-hour traffic. Besides, theoretically I'm a housemate. But in reality this is your house, your rules. Really, I'm just a guest. I need my independence, my own place—even if it's a room in my childhood home—my own life.' *My own man.* Her heart gave a painful lurch at that thought. She didn't want another man. She wanted Wil.

If she and Wil had never hugged, had never kissed, had never flirted about the possibilities of mind-blowing sex, she might have agreed to extend their housemate situation into the school term after she went back to work. But they had and the dynamic of their friendship had changed irrevocably.

'We could make it work,' he said.

'How? The reason I'm here is to help you with Nina. I'll be at school all day. How could that work?'

'I could hire a nanny for when I had to work, and you could help with Nina after you get home. You'd have the school holidays, too.'

'What if I want to go out after work? Or go away on the holidays? I'm already planning to go to Greece in the midwinter break. I need my own life, remember? I have to move on.'

'We must be able to reach a compromise.' He paused. 'Nina would really miss you. Sultan and Calypso would miss you. That orange cat would miss you.'

'And you, Wil?' She tried to make her voice light-hearted but it betrayed her by breaking. 'Would you miss me?'

He scowled his darkest Wil scowl. 'Do you have to ask that? Of course I'd miss you. Georgie, I want—'

Whatever he was going to say, she didn't hear it for the sudden chimes of music emanating from Nina's hammer. Georgia immediately glanced over to her charge; Wil did the same. Then he looked back to her. 'Nina got the hammer by herself,' he said.

Georgia jumped up from the sofa and clapped her hands. 'She crawled to get it by herself. On her belly and not very elegantly. But she crawled for the first time! Now she's off again. Look at her go. Oh, clever girl. She's going to be an athlete when she grows up. Where's the camera?'

'My phone is on the countertop.' Wil got up to get it. 'Another milestone to check off the list.'

'And many more to come. I'm so proud of her.'

Wil looked down at her. 'You care about Nina, don't you?'

There was little point in hiding the truth. 'Yes. I do. More than I could ever have imagined I would, even though I tried not to get attached.'

She thought back to what Jackie had said. That she would grow to love Nina because she was part of Wil. There was that. But it was more. Nina was a little person in her own right, with her own personality, quite independently of Wil. Georgia had come to care for her because she was Nina, not just because she was Wil's daughter. She wanted to be around to see her develop into a toddler right up to the teenager Wil joked about and beyond. To celebrate the milestones with Nina as someone important to her. Not just someone on her periphery. The idea of being her stepmother didn't seem as scary as it had.

Jackie's words came back to her. *'Because you love Wil, you'll learn to love and cherish his daughter.'* Had Jackie seen what she couldn't see for herself? She wasn't *falling* in love with Wil, something she could stop. She was already head over heels in love with her best friend. Totally and irrevocably.

Wil took photos and video of his daughter from every angle, urged on by a delighted Georgia. While pleased about his Nina's new mobility, he was more excited by what he'd seen in Georgia's eyes when she was watching Nina. Something that could change the course of their misaligned stars. Because he didn't really want a nanny for Nina. He wanted a mother.

And for himself?

He wanted Georgia.

Since she had moved in, this big, expensive house had become a home. A home full of the spirit, energy and generous heart of this beautiful person. All these years, she had been there right under his nose masquerading as his friend. When all along she had been his ideal woman. Deep down, he thought he'd always had an inkling that Georgia was 'The One'. Yet he'd resisted it, knowing he wasn't ready, promising himself *one day*.

That one day had crept up on him. This time, he was not going to easily let her go. Problem identified. Solution in progress. Plan of action to be determined. Pronto.

'Let me get a shot of you with Nina,' he said. 'I think she might have had enough of crawling.'

Her hands went to her head. 'My hair. It's a mess. The humidity.' Her hair had indeed gone off in all wavy directions. But he liked it. Ached to run his fingers through it, gently tug on it to tilt her head back for his kiss. This last week of the 'no touch' rule had been hell. If he had his way, that was about to change.

'Your hair looks great. It always looks great. *You* always look great.' She looked particularly good today in denim shorts and a peach-coloured blouse in that cotton lace stuff with tiny holes in it. There was a smear on the shoulder that looked like puréed carrot transferred by tiny fingers, but he didn't have the heart to tell Georgia. After all, the colour sort of co-ordinated.

She flushed and looked pleased. Did he pay

her enough compliments? Did she even realise that the friend-zone barriers were crumbling?

Georgia bent down to pick Nina up. Wil shot off a series of candid photos as she dropped a kiss on his daughter's downy little head without seeming to realise she was doing so, it had become so automatic when she was with Nina, before folding her into her arms. A huge surge of emotion swept over him at just how right his two favourite people looked together. No one seeing them together would disbelieve that Nina could belong to Georgia as much as to him. That they could be a real family. *His* family.

He'd never been one to curse and rail against the misery and injustice of his childhood. Resilience and sheer determination not to allow himself to be broken had seen him through. Then he'd hit the adoption jackpot with parents like Jackie and Dave, so how could he regret the rest? But those years in care, when survival was all he'd had on his mind, had stifled his ability to dream. Now, he found himself believing that finally the richness of the life that stretched ahead of him could make up for the aridity of the past. When Georgia suggested a selfie of the three of them, he had to swallow hard before he could manage a cheerful reply.

But it wasn't difficult to smile for the camera when he had his arm holding both Georgia and Nina close. He dared to dream that both of them were his.

All the excitement inevitably ended in tears from an exhausted and over-stimulated Nina. Georgia was rostered on baby duty and while Wil got Nina's bottle ready, Georgia was the one who gave it to her then took her to the nursery to settle her for her second nap of the day. Wil left her to it. He needed some time alone to strategise.

By the time Georgia came back—wearing a snug-fitting, clean white top that made no secret of the shape of her breasts—he was ready.

'She's out like a light,' she said.

'There's some stuff from the gourmet deli in the fridge for lunch, if you'd like to join me.' He tried to act like a housemate and not assume they would always eat together. Even though they'd shared every meal since Georgia had got here. He didn't want to be guilty of taking her company for granted. Far from it.

'Sounds good,' she said. 'But first, we really need to continue our discussion.'

'We do,' he said. 'I have a plan.' He looked down into her face. Knew he had to choose his words carefully. She might need convincing.

He didn't want to scare her off. Not when he wanted this so very much.

She raised her eyebrows. 'Really? So quickly? I'm all ears.'

'I think we should get married,' he said.

CHAPTER FOURTEEN

GEORGIA STARED UP at Wil. She felt the colour drain from her face and her mouth went dry. Her heart tripped into an erratic beating of anticipation. 'Wil, did you just propose to me?'

'It makes sense, doesn't it?' he said. 'That we get married, I mean. Checks all the boxes, in fact.'

'Boxes?' she said. She suspected that didn't include the type of tiny velvet box in which nestled a glittering engagement ring. Her heart commenced a slow, disappointed sinking from the heights of elation to which it had soared.

'We get on so well,' he said. 'You're my best friend. You like living here, I like having you here. You're the perfect mother for Nina. My family all think we're engaged already so we'd be continuing as expected.'

Her heart sank even further. She put up her hand. Noticed it trembled. 'Wait. You're proposing a fake marriage following on from our fake engagement?'

'Hell, no. I'm talking a real marriage. In every way. I think we both know we'd be okay in that, uh, department.'

Who was this person? So sober and stilted and totally lacking in spontaneity. *Where was Wil?* 'You mean, to be specific, in the mind-blowing sex department?'

'Exactly,' he said, without a hint of his devastating dimple.

Georgia waited for him to take her in his arms, to kiss her senseless and let her know exactly what she had to look forward to in her marriage bed. If that was indeed what he meant.

'Anything else to add? Another box?' *Had someone put him up to this?*

'It goes without saying that as, uh, my wife you'd be totally financially secure. You can be sure of that.'

'You're talking a pre-nuptial agreement?'

'Only if you want one. I trust you.'

Trust. What about *love*?

Her disappointment was so intense it threatened to choke her. 'You sound like you're setting out a business proposal. Not a proposal of marriage.'

'Does it sound like that? I didn't want you to

think this was a hastily constructed response to you wanting to move out. That it wasn't a genuine offer.'

'It's all very convenient, isn't it?' she said, trying to keep the edge of bitter disappointment from her voice, not sure she succeeded. 'Long-time schoolteacher friend slots in as mother for your child. The child you only recently acquired. It's like insta-family. Just add wife. Even more convenient as your parents approve. My parents would too, by the way. Everyone would be congratulating you on your excellent decision to secure me.' *Good old Georgia to the rescue—a lifetime of rescue.*

'I wouldn't put it like that,' he said with something like alarm in his eyes.

'How would you put it?' she said.

'That it would be a very good idea for you to marry me. For all concerned.'

Tell me you love me, Wil. Tell me you love me and I'll say yes.

But he didn't.

She took a deep, steadying breath that didn't do much to take the wobble out of her voice. 'In that case, I must respectfully decline your proposal.'

He stared at her for a long moment. She wasn't sure how to read the expression on his face. Disbelief. Disappointment. Surely not anguish.

'You're saying no,' he said.

'Yes. I mean *no*. I'm saying I don't think marriage to me is the solution to your problems.'

If only it could have been different.

She knew by saying no, she was waving goodbye to not only sharing her life with the man she loved, but also any hope of an ongoing friendship with him. How could they come back from this? All the ease that had marked their friendship would be gone for ever. She knew only too well how a man behaved towards a woman who had turned down his proposal.

Wil furrowed his brow. 'I can't change your mind? Georgie, I think we'd have a great life if we got married. We'd be happy. Think of the fun we could have. You. Me. Nina. The horses.'

Just tell me you love me.

Crickets.

Georgia sighed. You couldn't force a person to love you. If she pursued the issue, of course he would parrot the words she wanted to hear, to get what he wanted. A convenient wife and a mother for Nina. But she wanted the real thing. One hundred per cent. Not second best. Not second thoughts. That was all she'd ever wanted. Georgia, who should have been George, was never going to settle for less.

'Wil, I'm sorry I can't give you the answer you want. It would have solved a lot of problems.' She gave a short, mirthless laugh. 'Not the least of which would be somewhere for me to live.'

'But you have a home here.'

'That's kind of you, but you know I can't stay. Not even until the start of term. I'm sorry to leave you in the lurch with Nina. But I actually think it's best for me to leave now.'

He caught her arm with his hand. She stilled. 'Don't go like this,' he said.

Don't propose like this, she thought. *Take me in your arms, tell me you love me and I'll stay.*

When she didn't reply, he dropped his hand from her arm.

'I'm not going to pack my bags and make the big dramatic exit,' she said, looking at a slight discolouration in the marble tile of the floor, ironically in the shape of a heart. If she met his gaze, she knew she would cry. 'But I don't think I should stay here tonight. It would be too awkward. I'm going to check in to a hotel. The big one by the beach in Manly if I can get a room. Give us some space. Then come back for my stuff tomorrow. And to say goodbye to Nina.' The thought of losing Nina from her life made her want to double over with pain.

Her parents' house was not an option. She couldn't endure the questions and demands for explanations. And the good friends she could have called on for a spot on their sofas were all away for the holidays.

'Nobody is asking you to go, Georgie.' There was such an edge of sadness to his voice that for a moment she wondered should she reconsider. Give up her dream of reciprocal head-over-heels love to accept what Wil was offering. But she would never be happy with compromising her heart.

'It's my choice. No hard feelings, Wil.'

She couldn't, wouldn't, kiss him goodbye. That would be just too painful. Not when she yearned for so much more from him. 'I'll let myself out,' she said as she turned and headed to her room to pack an overnight bag.

Wil followed Georgia to the front door, despite her refusal of his offer to carry her backpack to the car. She didn't say anything as she walked out; he raised his hand in farewell. He stood behind the solidly closed doors, heard her car take off down the driveway, the skid on the gravel when she stopped for the gates, the clang of the gates closing behind her.

Feeling as if he were pushing his way through fog, he made his way to the family room. The empty room where such a short time ago, in what already seemed another world, her laughter had pealed around the walls.

He heard a scratching sound, turned to see the ginger cat with its paw plaintively up against the outside of the glass sliding door. Looking for Georgia. The cat had never come up to the house before. But it knew, in that instinctive way of animals, that she had gone. 'Sorry, mate, she's abandoned us all,' Wil said.

Then slammed his hand on the back of the sofa so hard the pain jarred all the way up his arm. He cursed long and hard and viciously, his anger aimed at himself.

He had completely stuffed up the proposal that was meant to secure Georgia as his wife. It was as if his brain had planned to say one thing, his mouth had decided on a different pathway. He had wanted to tell Georgia how much she meant to him, how happy he would be if she would share her life with him. Instead he had blurted out a business proposal. All the solution on offer without any of the joy. Without any of the *love*.

No wonder his beloved friend had looked at him as if he were a stranger. No wonder he had lost her.

Did his inability to express what he really felt, how much he loved her, track back to his blighted childhood where to show love was to risk showing weakness that could be exploited? Had he got so good at wearing the mask of indifference he couldn't rip it off? That was no excuse. He was an adult now. He knew better.

Wil slammed the back of the sofa again. In doing so, he dislodged something hidden under one of the cushions. Georgia's sketchbook. She always snapped it shut when he came near. He'd teased her about what she could possibly have to hide about her lizard.

The book had fallen open when it had been dislodged. Not a drawing of a lizard but an exquisite sketch of Nina's face in repose. So skilfully rendered, it brought his daughter to life on the paper. Beautiful. Innocent. Precious. He stared at the front of the book and flicked through every page. All drawings of Nina. Some of the images weren't finished, as if Georgia had been interrupted or Nina had demanded her attention. He stopped on a sketch of him looking down into Nina's face and her looking up at him. Just like the mo-

ment when he had recognised his mama in his
baby's eyes and Nina had seemed to recognise
him. It made the hairs on the back of his neck
stand up. This had been drawn with compas-
sion and love. For Nina. For *him*.

He'd made such a terrible mistake. Let
something of inestimable value slip through
his fingers. *The woman he loved.* And who
might love him. When he'd suggested marriage, he'd hoped she would learn to love him.
This picture gave him hope.

He had to go find her. Bare his heart to her.
Get right back into grovelling mode and grovel
for his life. Carefully, he put Georgia's sketchbook back under the cushion. Then stopped as
he heard the front door open and close, and
Georgia's footsteps—already so familiar—
tap their way down the hallway towards him.

Georgia had barely got to the end of Wil's
street when she had realised she had to turn
back. *Wil was her friend.* She couldn't leave
him like that, with pain and bewilderment in
his eyes. Not after all the awful things that
had happened to him in his life. The people
who had let him down. In that tall, power-
fully built, successful wealthy man was still
the soul of the five-year-old boy on the beach,
the thirteen-year-old white knight who'd saved

the damsel in distress and been thrown into a dungeon for his pains.

All that time he'd been checking off the boxes, she'd been silently urging him to tell her he loved her. But she hadn't said a word about love. She'd been knocked for six by his sudden suggestion of marriage—she really couldn't call it a proposal—but couldn't she have come out and said, *What about love, Wil?* Instead of *thinking* it and expecting him to read her mind?

She was going to march down that hallway and tell him how she felt about him, and how she wished he felt about her. If she didn't like what she heard in response, at least she would have tried and could walk away without regrets.

Then he was there, in front of her. 'You came back,' he said hoarsely. 'I was about to set off to find you.'

He held out his arms and she didn't hesitate to go into them. *Wil.* As she snuggled in against his chest, her head against his shoulder and his arms tight around her, she felt as if she was coming home. She stood there for what seemed like an age, eyes closed in sheer relief, breathing in the intoxicating, familiar scent of him, rejoicing that she was there, *loving him.*

Finally, when she could feel the tension between them ease, the relief that they had found each other, she pulled back. Resting against the circle of his arms, she looked up at his face. He smiled and she smiled back.

'Remember how we sorted out our last problem? About me moving here, I mean?' she said. 'Perhaps we could try that again.'

'You mean, you tell me I need to tell you how much I love you?' he said.

'Sounds like a plan,' she said with a slow smile and a heart soaring to elation from the unfathomable depths to which it had plunged.

'Then I say, "Georgia, I love you. I've always loved you, since the moment I saw you standing there in the university quadrangle, stamping your foot because there wasn't an equestrian club."'

She reached up and kissed him on the mouth. 'Really? That far back? Was I truly stamping my foot?'

'With your dainty riding boot.'

'I'm not sure I believe you. About the boot, I mean. But I'll take the way-back-then love.'

He laughed and she delighted in the sound of it. Wil deserved so much laughter in his life.

'Now let me continue,' she said. 'Then I tell you, that all I want is to be head over heels in love with the man I marry.'

'And then I ask you, "Georgia, are you head over heels in love with me?"' Wil's tone was light-hearted, in keeping with their game, but his eyes told her that her answer was important.

'And I say…' Her voice started to break and she had to swallow the lump in her throat before she could continue. 'I say, yes. I am totally head over heels in love with you, Wil Hudson. And I'm glad. You see, I was beginning to worry that I couldn't love, that I was incapable of loving a man. Now I realise it's because of you. *It was always you.* I couldn't love another man because there wasn't room in my heart. It was already full of love for you. I just didn't recognise it.'

This time he kissed her, a passionate possession of her mouth. The kiss was long and sweet and full of promise. Finally they came up for breath. Wil was first to speak. 'Now you pose the question to me: is my love for you the head-over-heels kind? The kind where I pick you up and whirl you round and declare myself?'

'Well, are you? Will you? Do the whirl thing, I mean?'

Wil didn't reply, but rather put his hands around her waist, picked her up and whirled her around the room until she was breathless and laughing. 'I'm head over heels, crazy in love with you, Georgia Lang. Will you marry me?'

She didn't hesitate. 'Yes, Wil, yes. I will marry you.' She wasn't sure whether she was giddy from the whirling, or delirious with joy. Then she got a little more giddy from the passion of Wil's kiss as he held her tight.

'Now for the ring,' he said. 'A proper head-over-heels-type proposal of marriage is always accompanied by a ring.'

'You wouldn't have had time to buy a ring and I wouldn't expect—'

He pulled out a little black velvet box from the side pocket of his trousers. Then flipped open the lid to reveal an exquisite vintage emerald and diamond ring.

Georgia gasped. 'Your grandmother's ring. But how—?'

'Ned brought it up with him from Five and a Half Mile Creek. Gave it to me at the christening.'

'You didn't say anything.'

'I was waiting for the right moment. Do you like it? If not, I can get you another ring more to your taste. Or we can have the stones remodelled into something more contemporary.'

'I love it just the way it is. It's utterly perfect. And I love what it represents too. The love of your family for you.'

Wil took her left hand. 'I wonder will it fit?' He slid it onto her third finger. 'Yes. Perfectly. Meant to be. Good karma, remember.'

Georgia splayed her hand and held it away from her to admire her engagement ring, the way it caught the light and glittered. She sighed from sheer joy. 'I never want to take it off.'

'What do you think of an Easter wedding at Five and a Half Mile Creek?'

She looked up to his beloved face. 'Perfect. Thank you, Wil. Thank you for everything. Thank you for Nina. I love her too, as if I had borne her. And I promise to always be a good mother to her.'

'I know you will,' he said. 'And to any sisters or brothers we might give her.'

She kissed him for that. A kiss of affirmation that rapidly escalated into something more insistent that sent desire throbbing through her. 'Wil, about that mind-blowing sex?'

'Yes,' he said, nuzzling her neck so she murmured in pleasure.

'Your room or mine?'

'Definitely mine,' he said. 'Shall your head-over-heels husband-to-be pick you up and carry you to the bed?'

'Why not start as we mean to continue?'

she said, as he lifted her up and into his arms. 'With love and passion and a whole lot of fun.'

'I'm looking forward to marrying my best friend,' he said.

'Me too,' she said. 'Friend, lover, husband.'

'Put *adoring* in front of those and you have me to a tee,' he said with a dimple-revealing grin.

She smiled. 'We're going to have such a wonderful life together.'

'Count on it,' he said.

* * * * *

Georgia thought, but how could she protest? She had the uncomfortable feeling she was being steamrollered, even if it was for the best of reasons.

'What about your family, Georgia?' said Jackie. 'It will be short notice for them. Do you think they will be able to attend the christening?'

Georgia stared at her, unable to speak. Her throat closed over. 'My family?' she managed to choke out. 'Oh, I...er...don't think so.'

'They may want to see their step-grand-daughter christened,' Jackie said.

Step-granddaughter? Of course, they would be Nina's step-grandparents. If this were for real.

Wil came to the rescue. 'We hadn't actually thought that far ahead.'

Georgia had no intention of telling her family anything about the fake engagement. She'd hoped she could keep it confined to Ingleside. This was in serious danger of spiralling out of control.

If her mother thought she was engaged to Wil, she'd cancel a court case to be there and meet his family. Her sisters would be agog. They always teased her that she'd let Wil— who they were convinced was her Mr Right—

get away. Once they knew, half of Sydney would know.

'We only want a very small ceremony, Mum,' said Wil. 'Ideally, just you, Dad, me and Georgie. That's what I want.' Georgia could see him improvising as he went along. 'For one thing, it would be in bad taste to have anything other than to keep it very small and very private when you consider it's so soon after Angie's death. I know we were divorced, but just out of respect. That's my final word.'

'I agree with Wil, of course,' said Georgia. In this case she most certainly did.

Jackie nodded. 'I can see your reasoning behind that decision. Small and private it shall be.'

Georgia looked to Wil and smiled, hoping she was masking her intense relief. He smiled back. Crisis averted.

But Jackie hadn't finished. 'But I'll need to get in touch with your parents anyway, Georgia,' she said. 'After all, we'll all want to pull together to organise the wedding. Have you two set a date?'

CHAPTER TEN

LATER THAT EVENING Wil was alone with Georgia in his bedroom. Not so much a bedroom but a luxurious hotel-like suite with the finest of furnishings in muted neutrals. His mother had pulled out all the stops on the master bedroom when they'd redecorated the house. Wil shut the door firmly behind him and Georgia to ensure their privacy. Nina's room was the next down the corridor; the bedroom his parents were sharing at the other end.

'What a day,' exclaimed Georgia, laughing, whirling around to face him. 'Your mum! She's a darling, but she never stops.'

'Never stops trying to organise my life, you mean,' he said, his tone mildly exasperated yet not masking his love for his mother. 'And now yours.'

'The look on your face when she asked us had we set a wedding date—I nearly cracked up,' said Georgia.

'Coming on top of the urgency of the christening, I'd really had enough, much as I love her,' he said.

'I couldn't look at you or I would have laughed out loud when you laid down the law. When you told her in such a controlled voice that we'll get married in our own good time—and that it wouldn't be until after she comes back from Italy.'

'I really had to grit my teeth when she suggested we might consider a destination wedding in Tuscany and that, if we liked, she could set the wheels in motion while she was over there.'

'I had to stop myself getting excited about that one. I mean, if it were real, if we really were getting married. Tuscany.'

'I didn't want to get cranky with her, but I'd had enough. I'm not as good at creating fibs on the spot as I thought I would be.'

'That's actually a good thing, Wil,' she said. 'I'm not a natural-born liar either. It's exhausting.'

'Mum kept us both on the spot,' he said. 'But you played your part so well, Georgie. I'm having another grovelling with gratitude moment.'

Wil threw himself down on one of the upholstered armchairs that were arranged around